RUNAWAY

Cordell Barker

Adapted by
Sarah Howden

National Film Board of Canada Collection

FIREFLY BOOKS

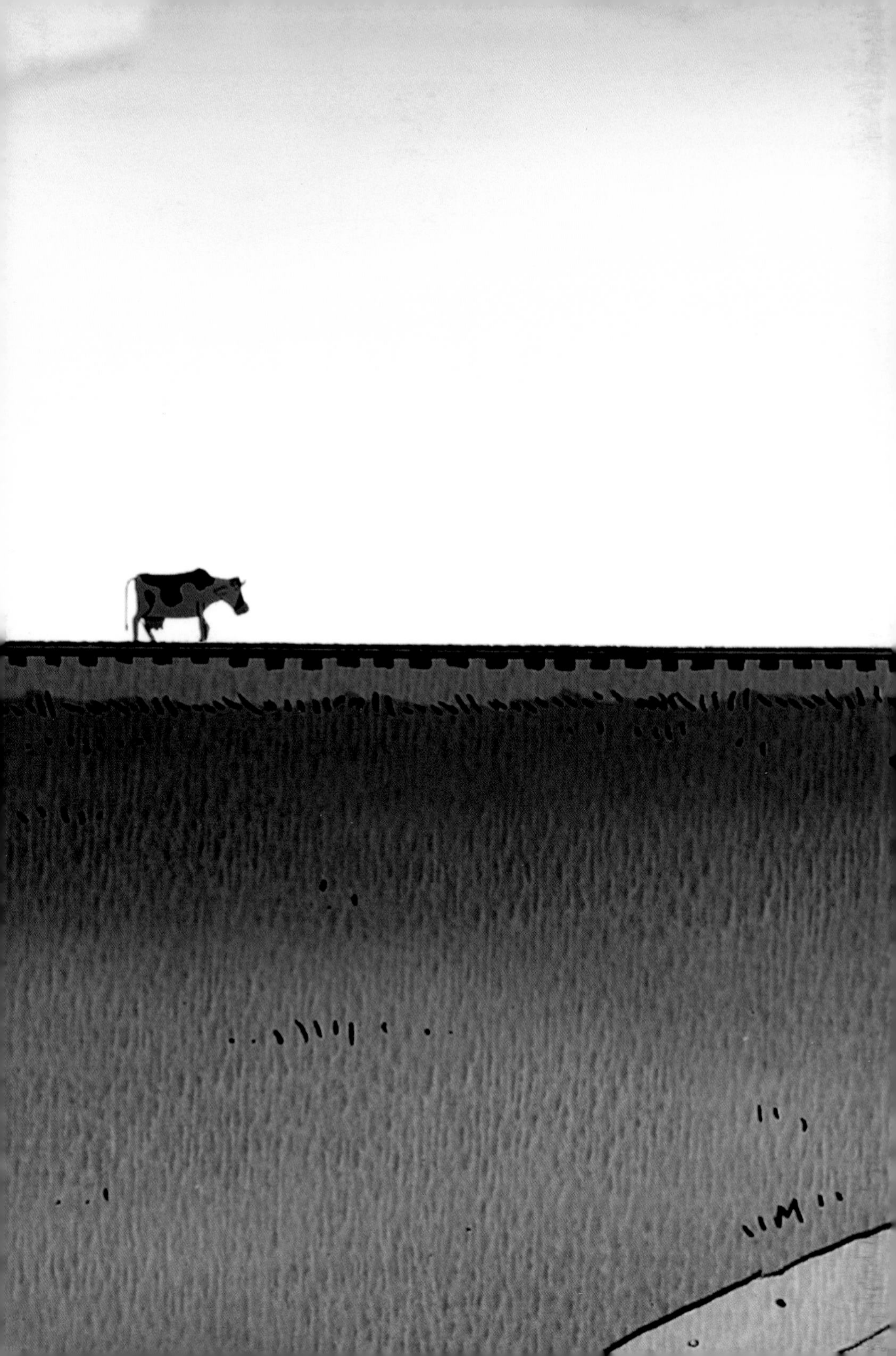

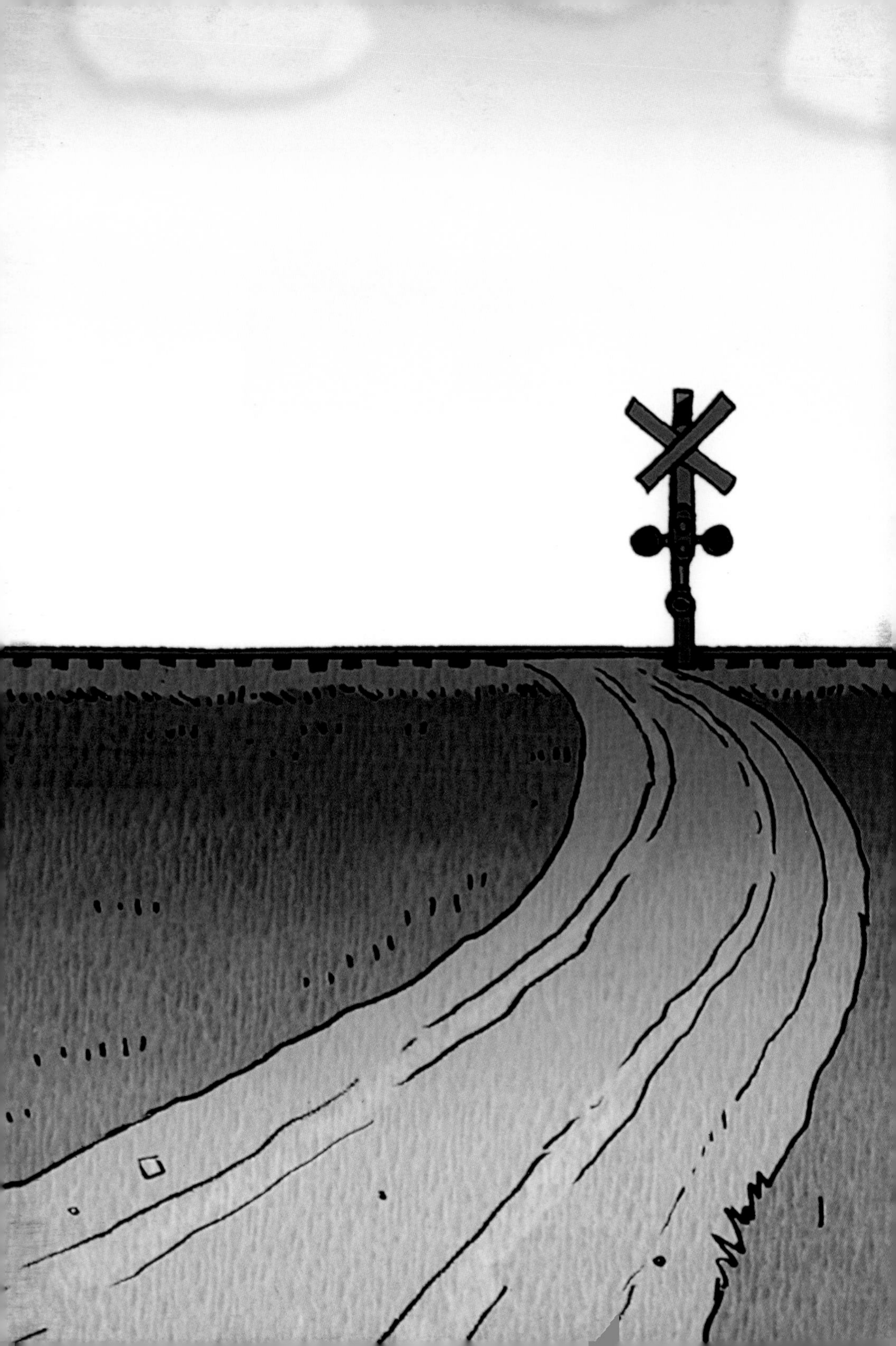

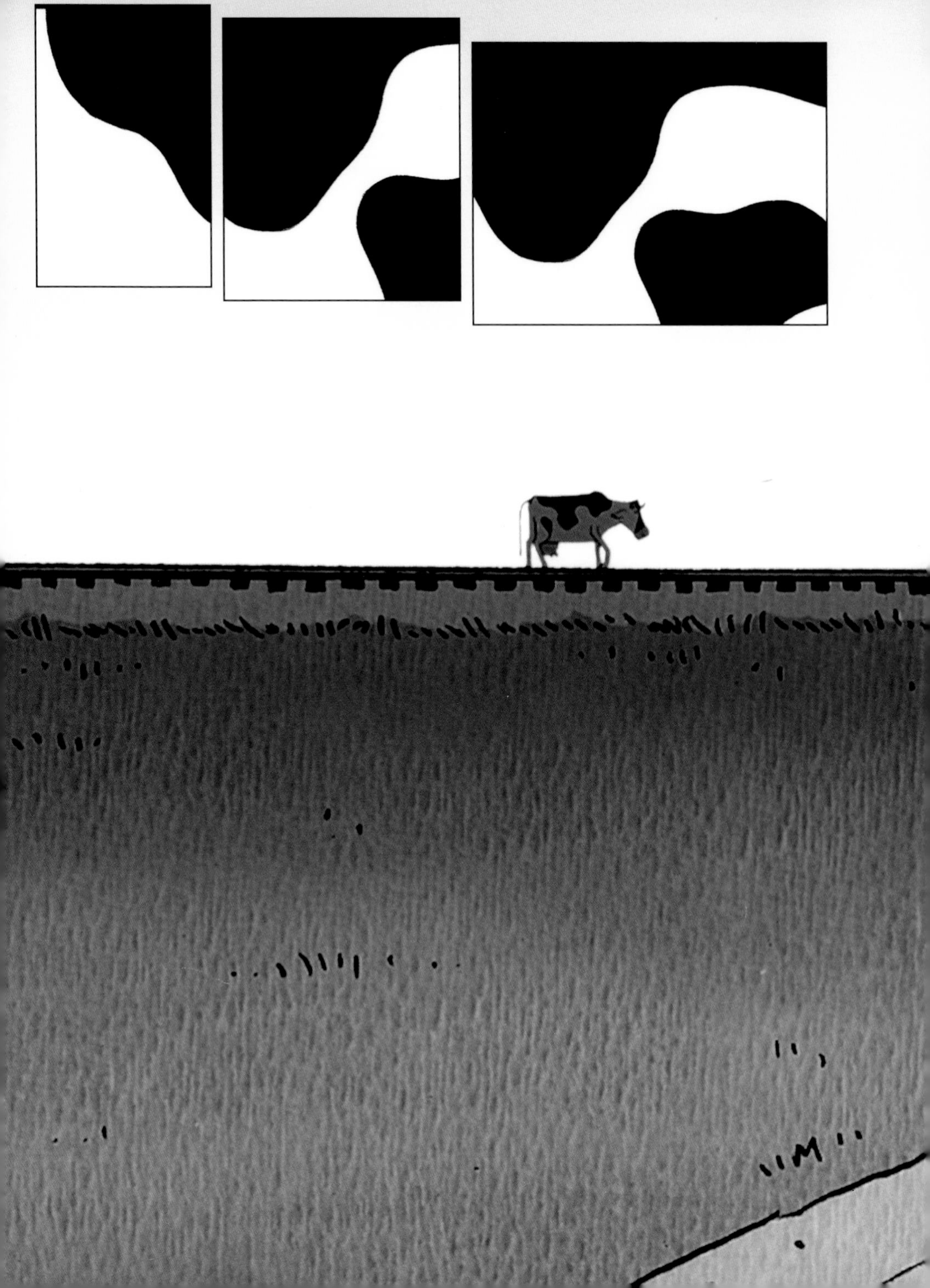

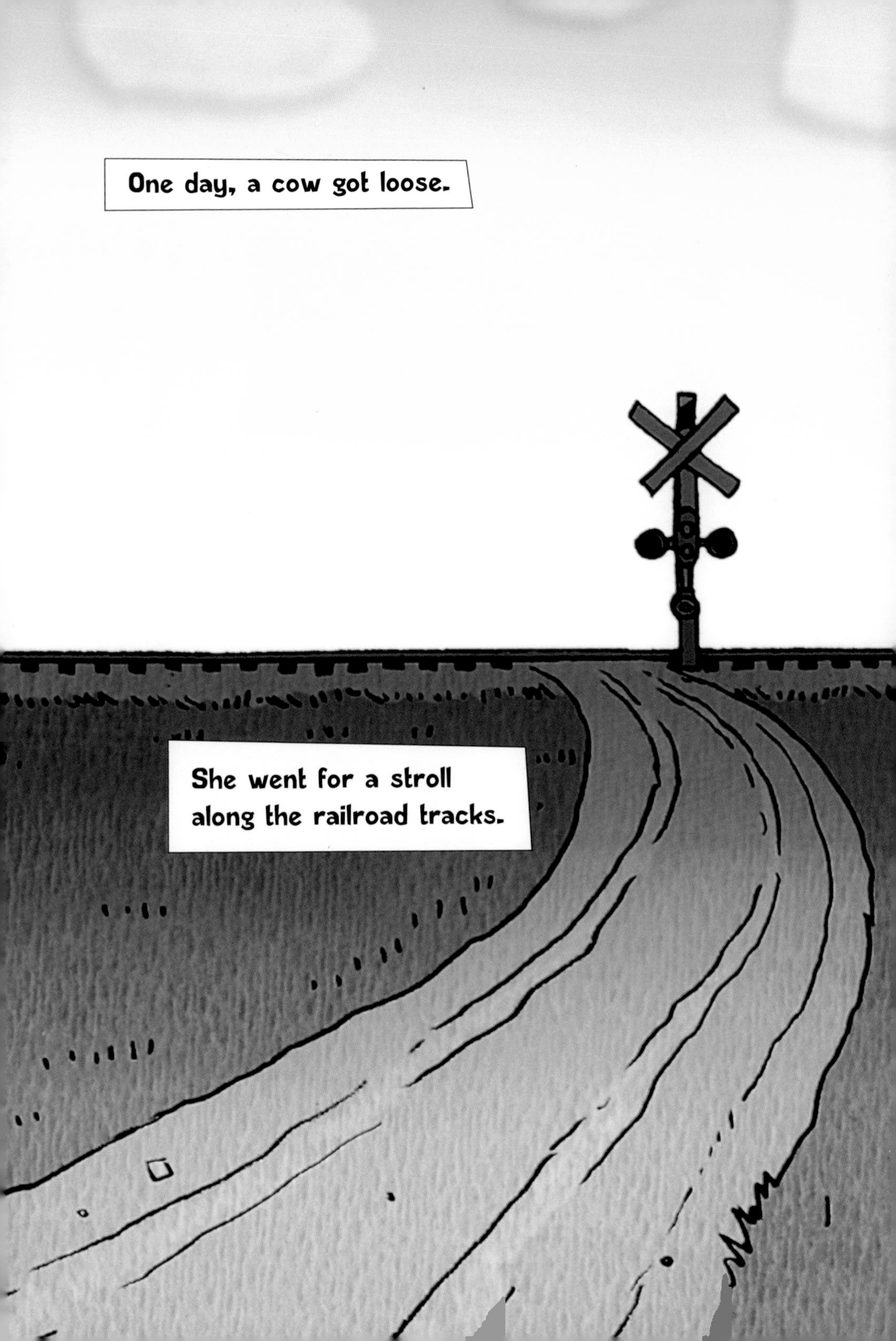
One day, a cow got loose.
She went for a stroll along the railroad tracks.

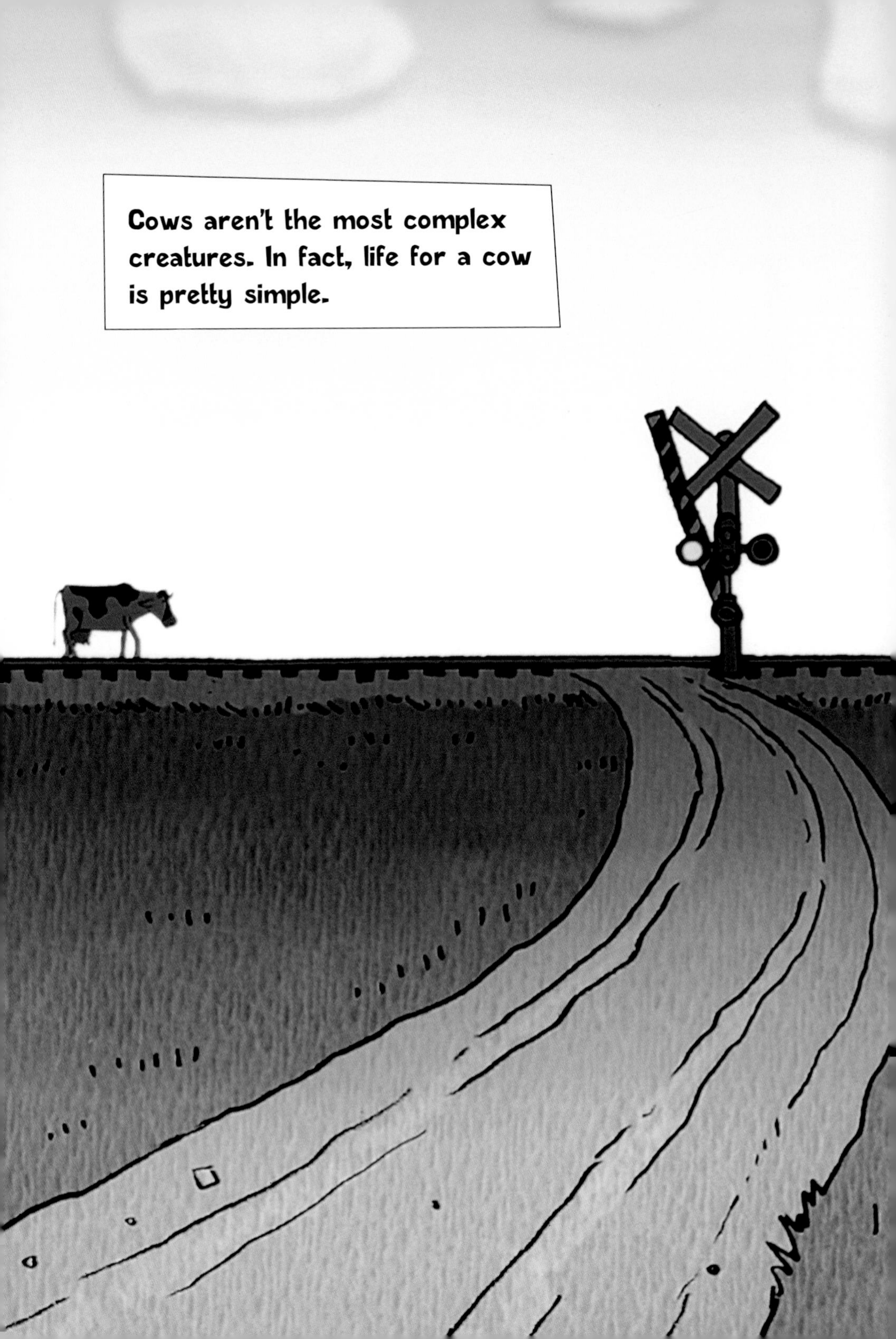
Cows aren't the most complex creatures. In fact, life for a cow is pretty simple.

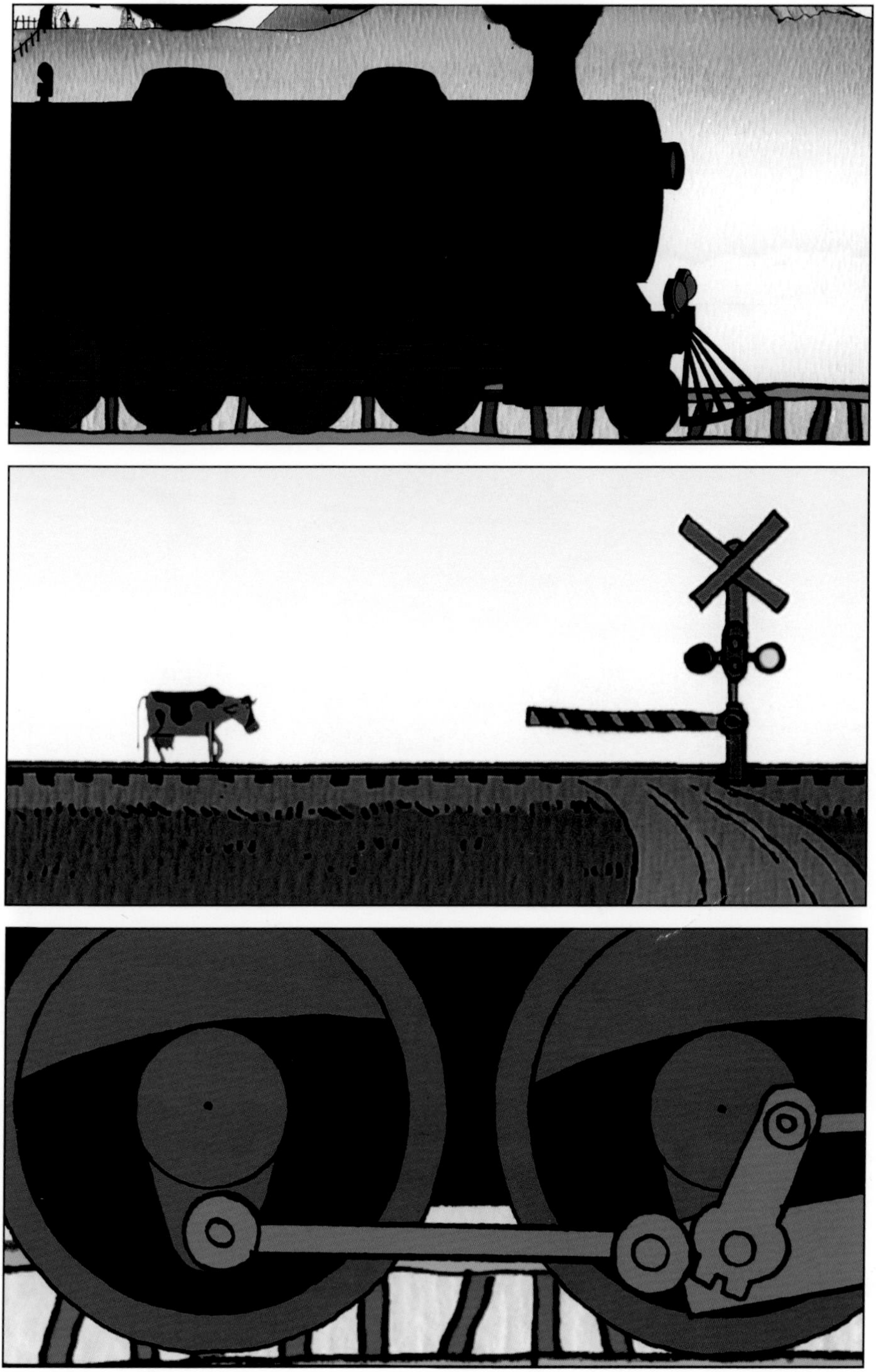

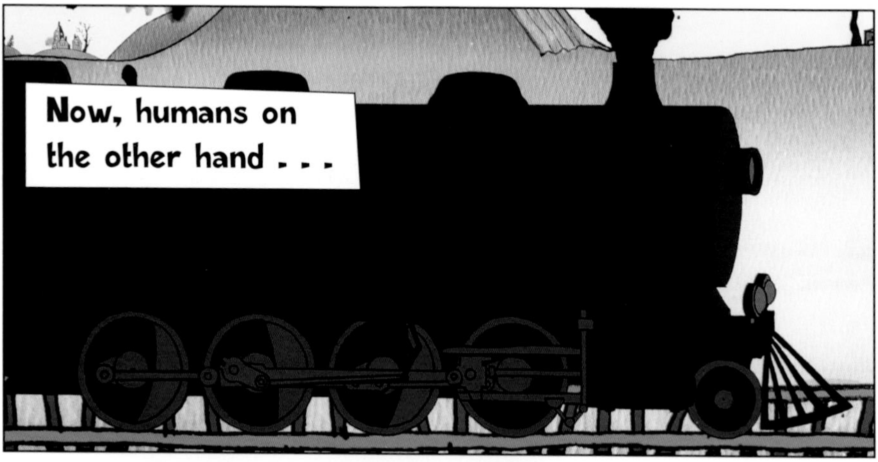
Now, humans on the other hand . . .

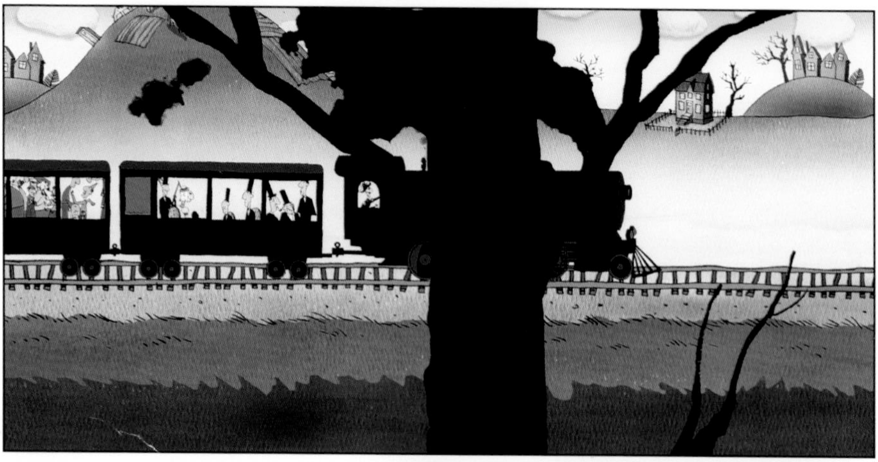

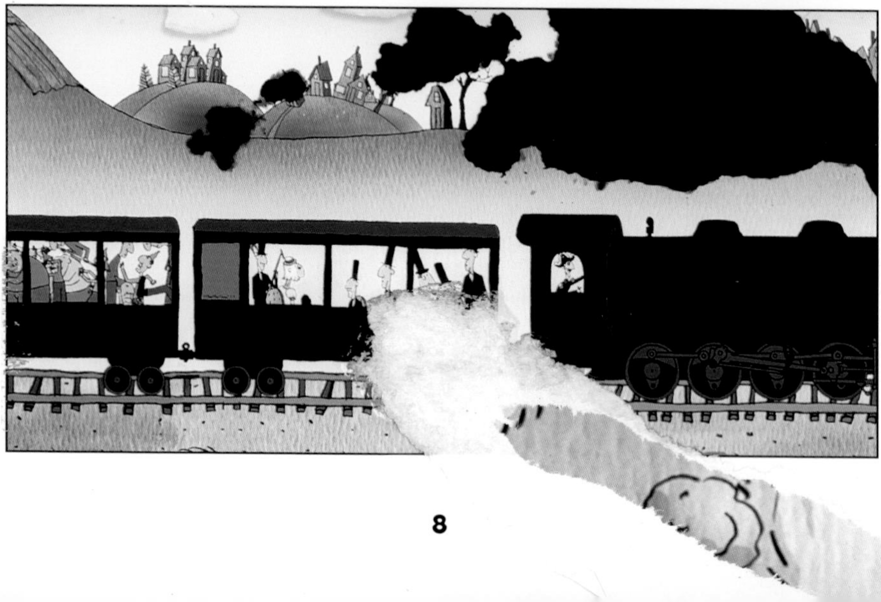

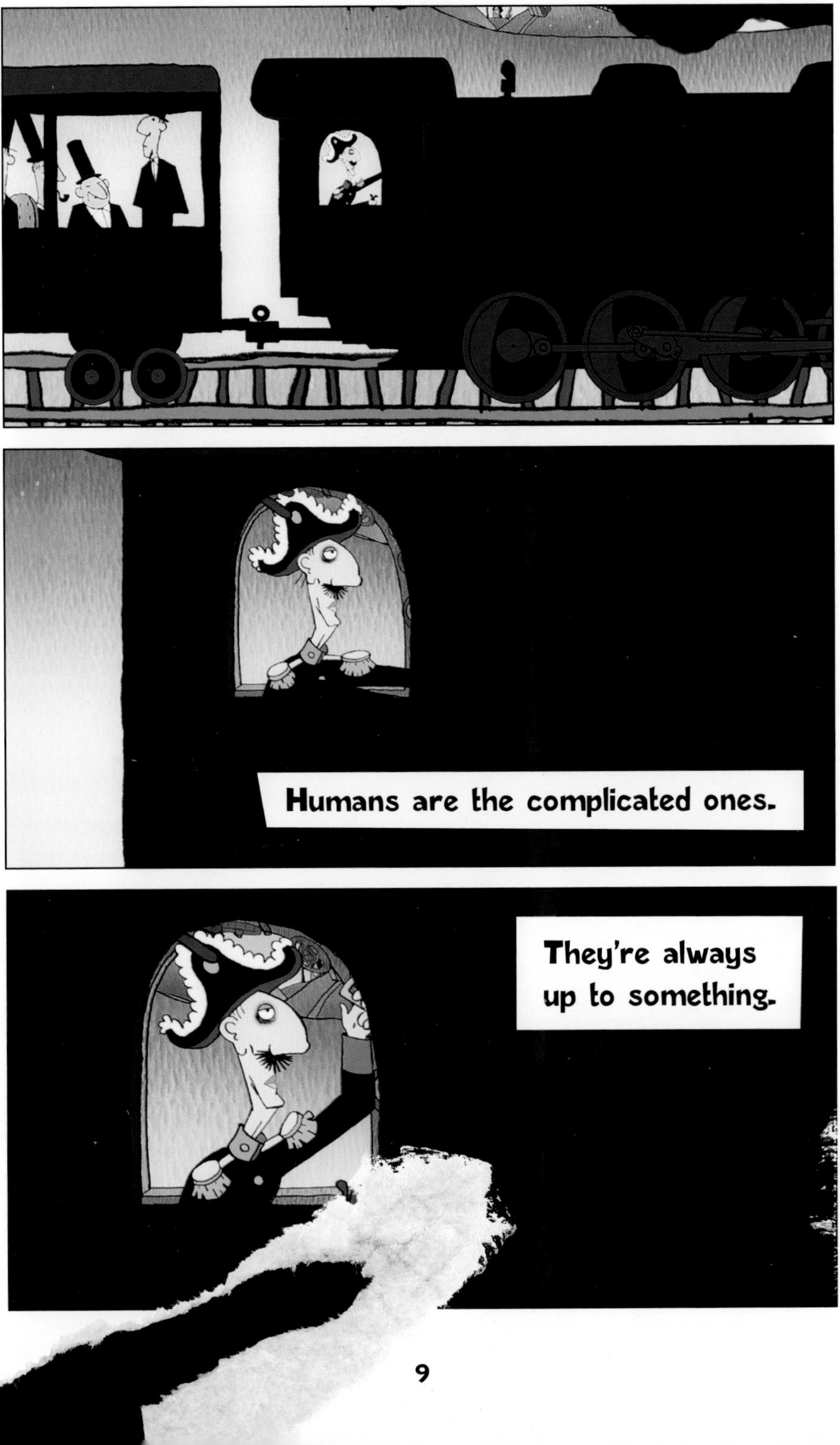
Humans are the complicated ones.
They're always up to something.

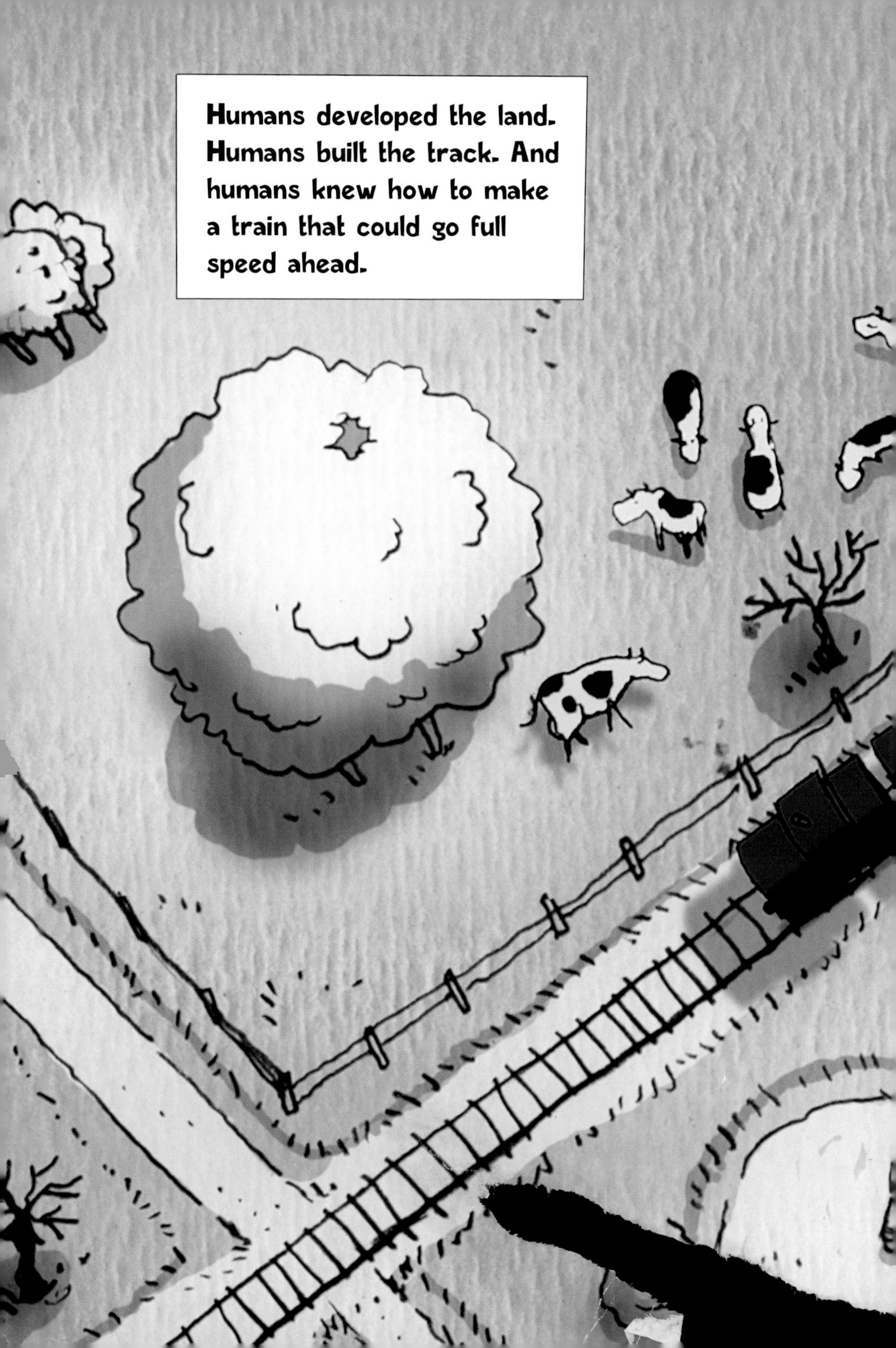
Humans developed the land. Humans built the track. And humans knew how to make a train that could go full speed ahead.

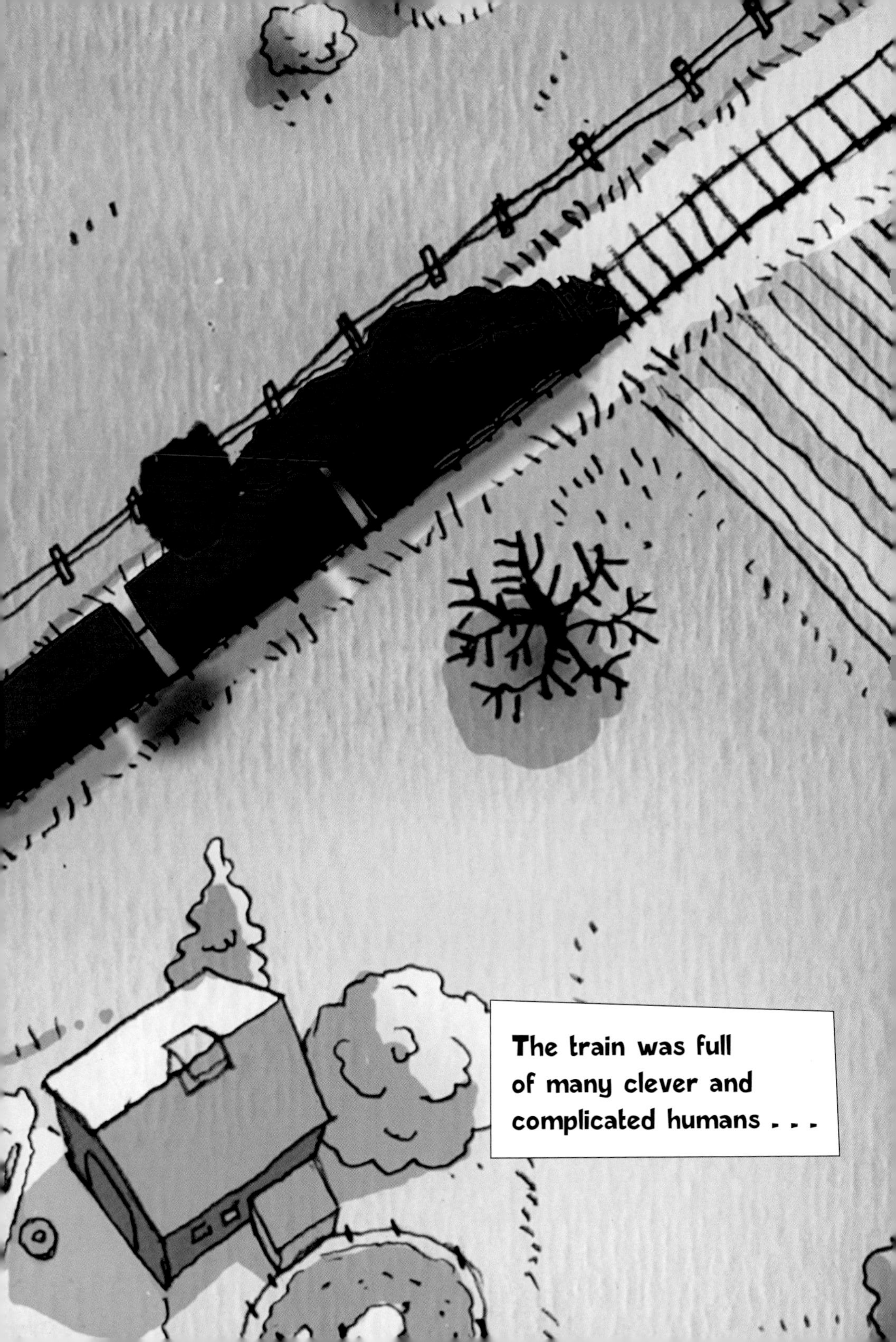
The train was full of many clever and complicated humans . . .

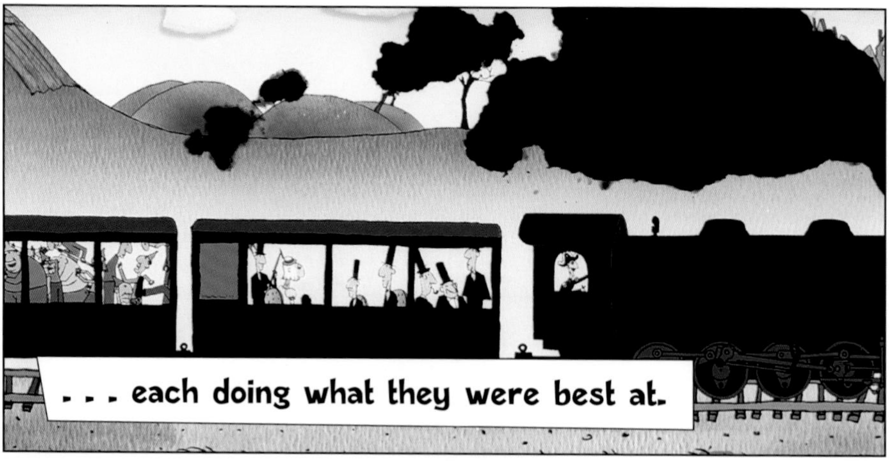
. . . each doing what they were best at.

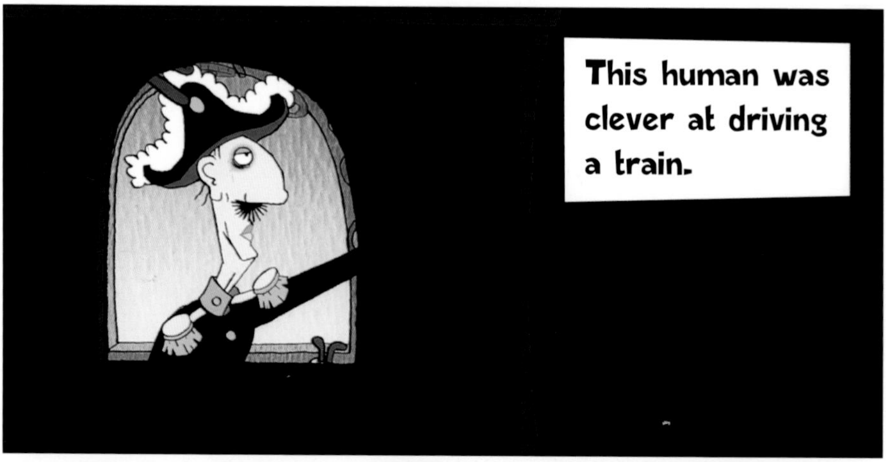
This human was clever at driving a train.

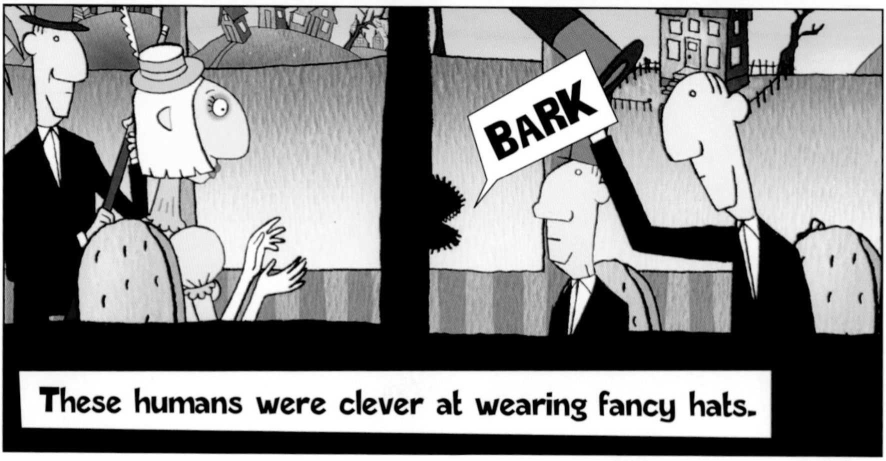
BARK
These humans were clever at wearing fancy hats.

These humans were clever at making good use of limited space.

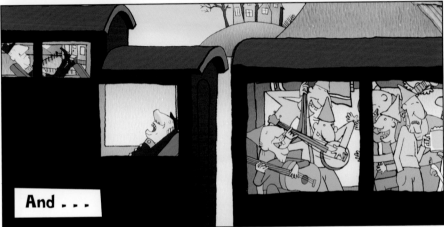

And . . .

. . . these humans were clever at sleeping.

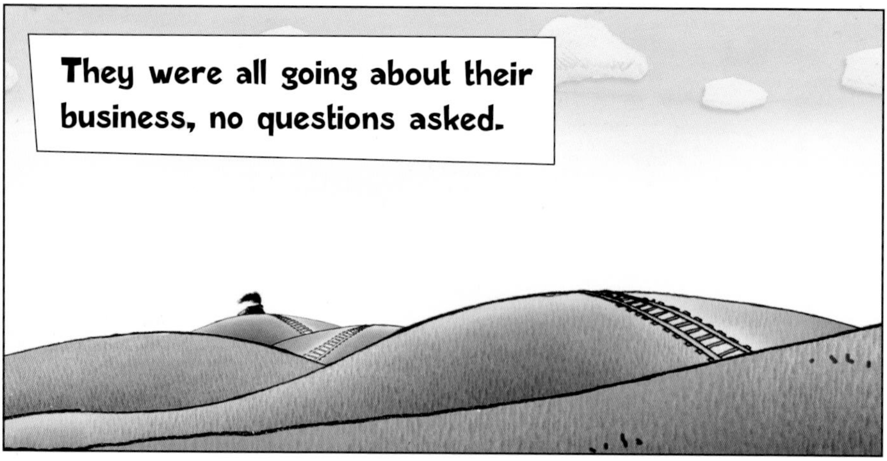
They were all going about their business, no questions asked.

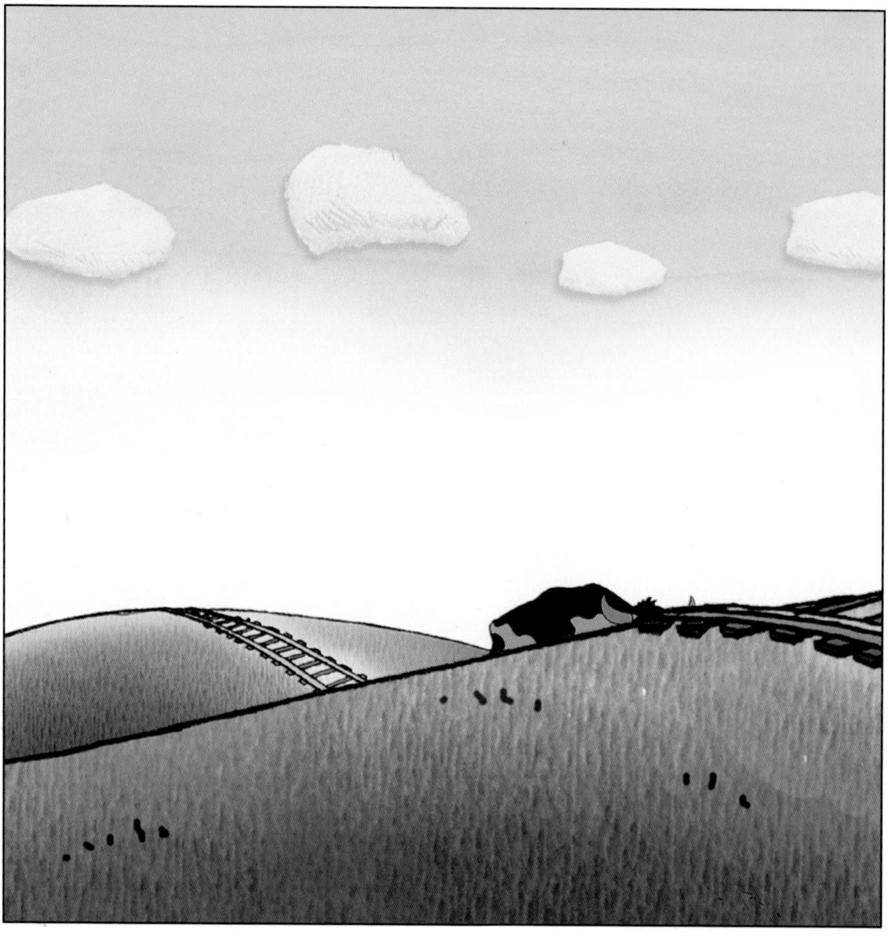

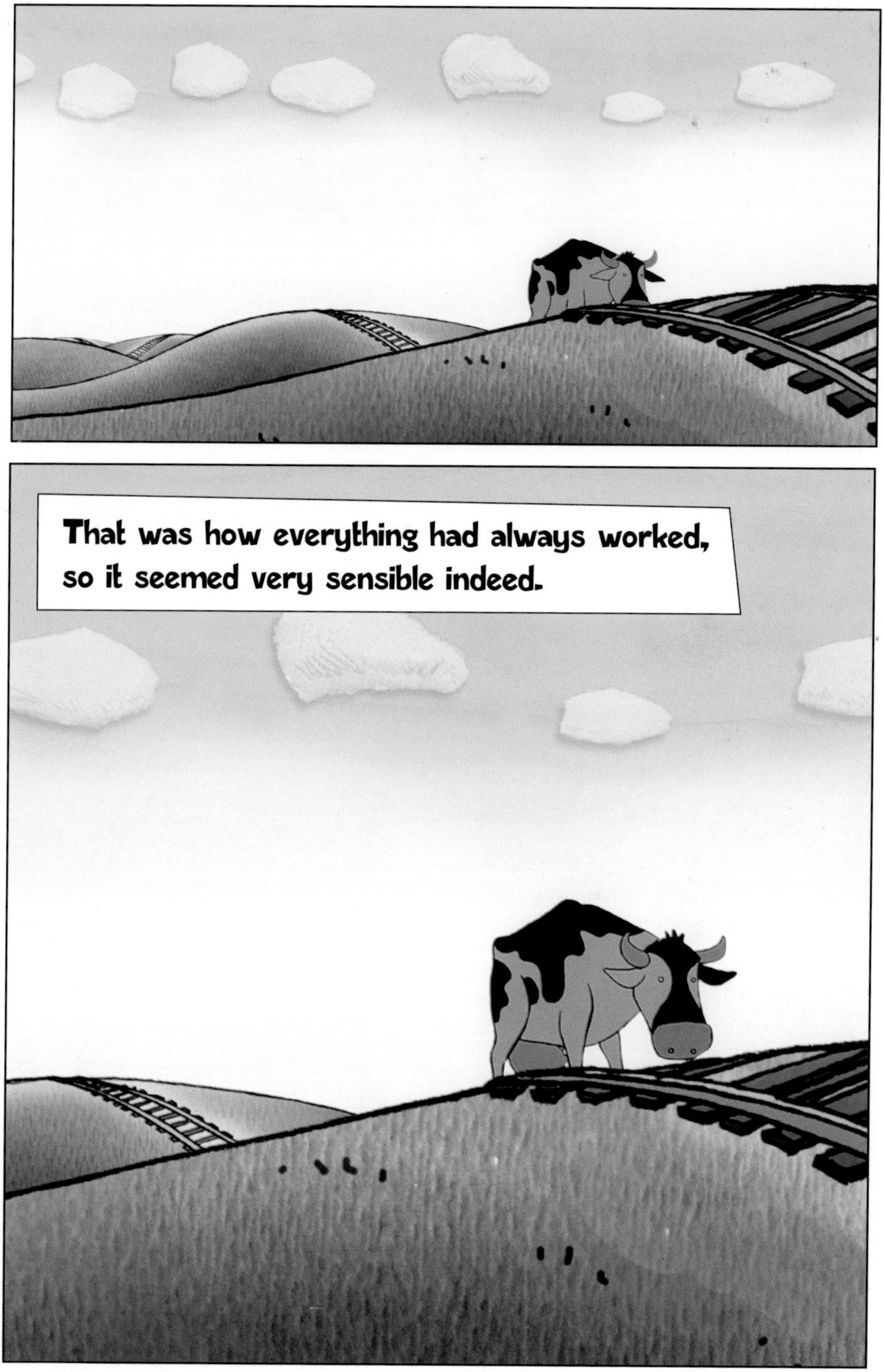
That was how everything had always worked, so it seemed very sensible indeed.

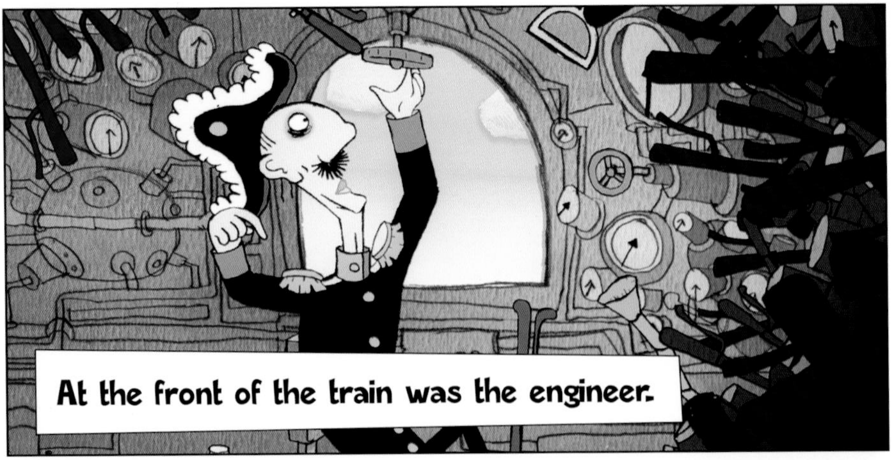
At the front of the train was the engineer.

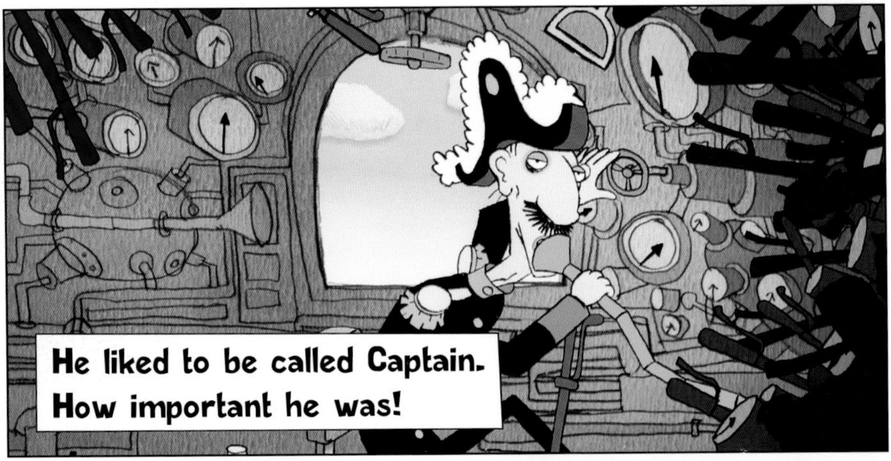
He liked to be called Captain.
How important he was!

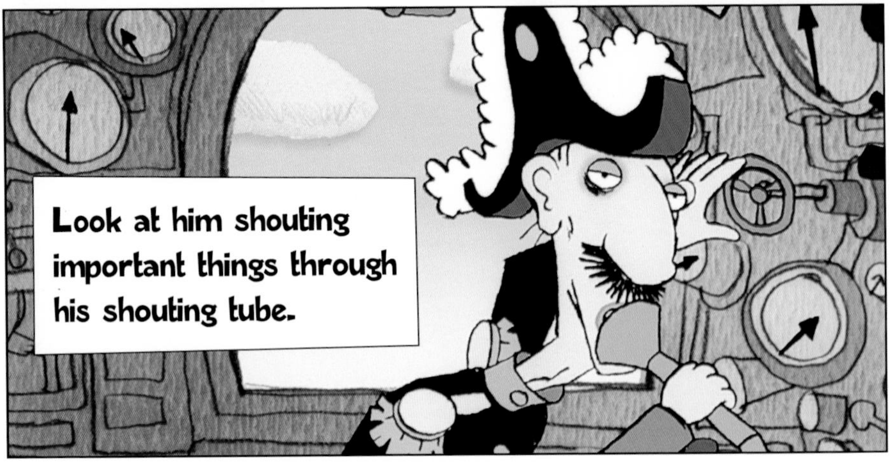
Look at him shouting
important things through
his shouting tube.

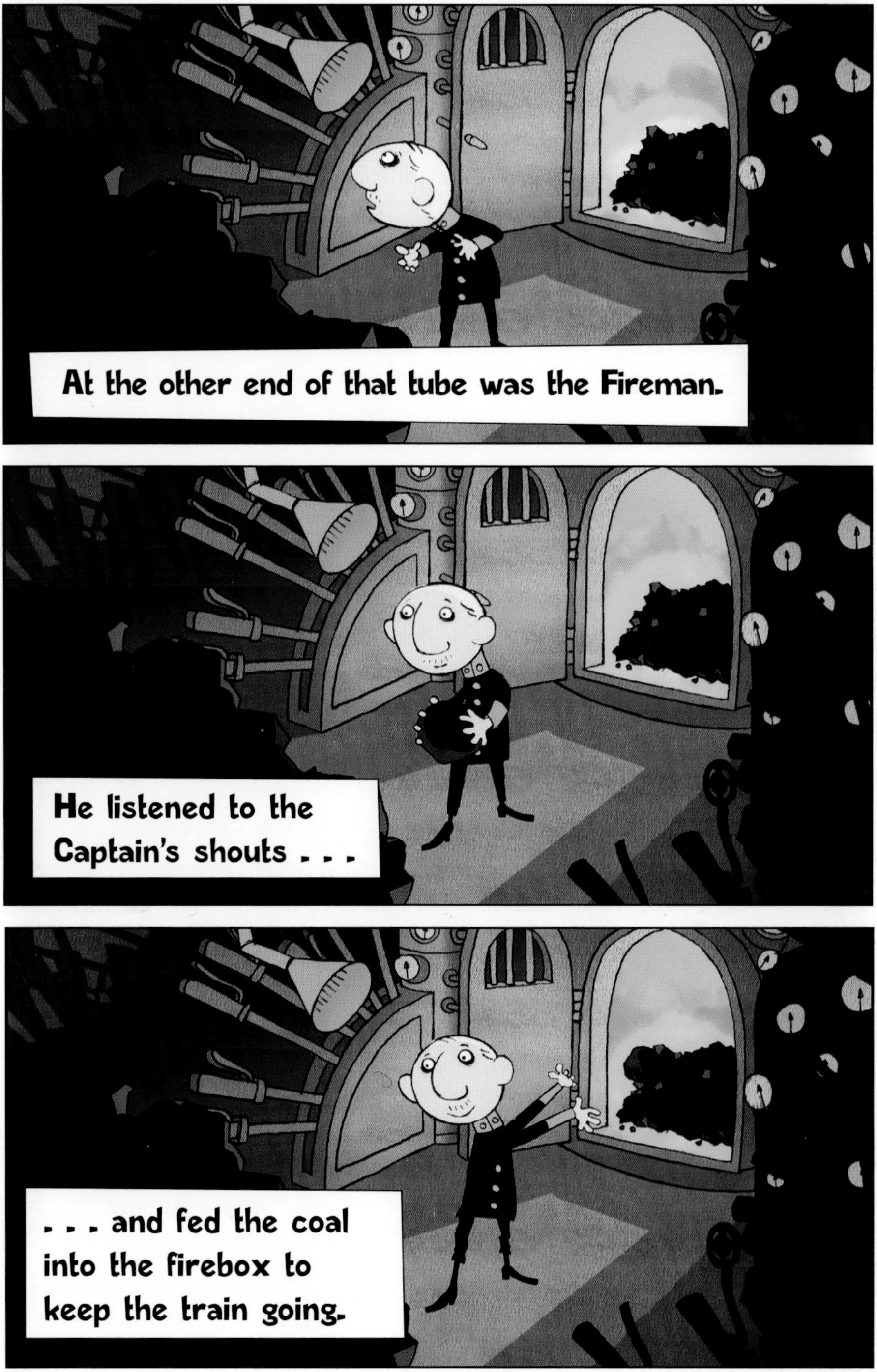
At the other end of that tube was the Fireman.
He listened to the Captain's shouts . . .
. . . and fed the coal into the firebox to keep the train going.

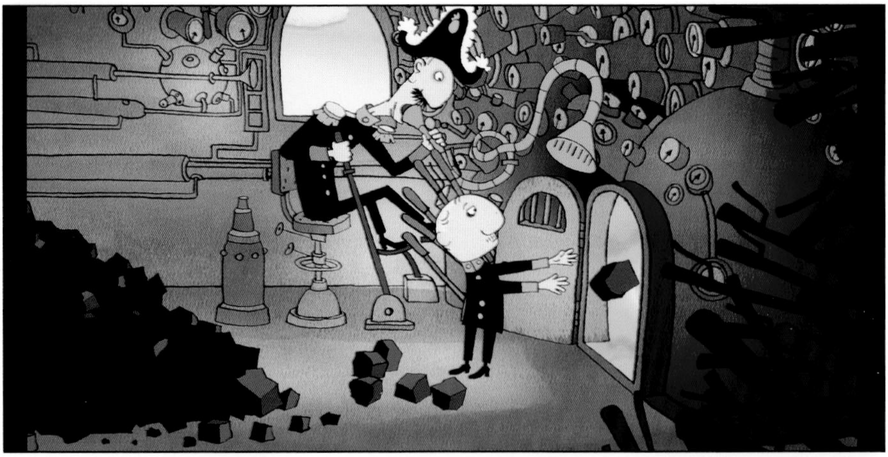

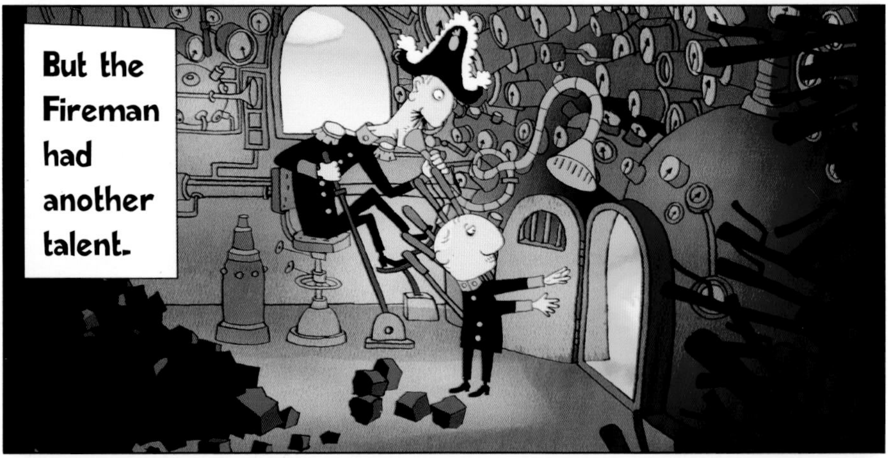
But the Fireman had another talent.

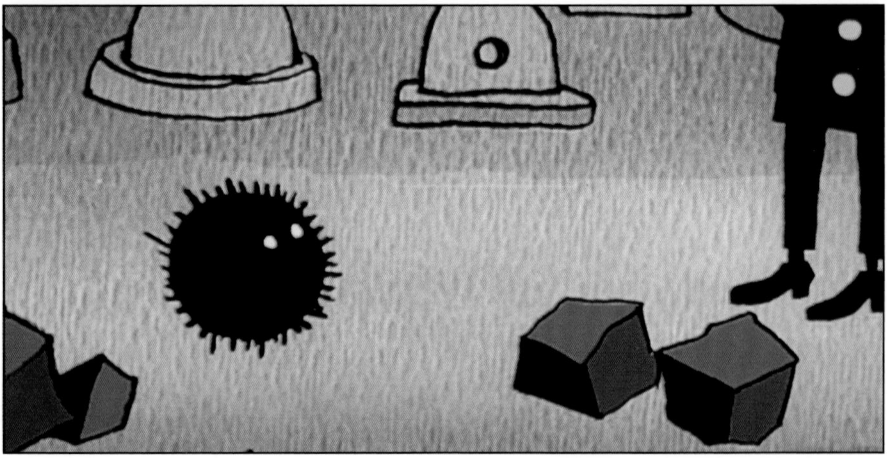

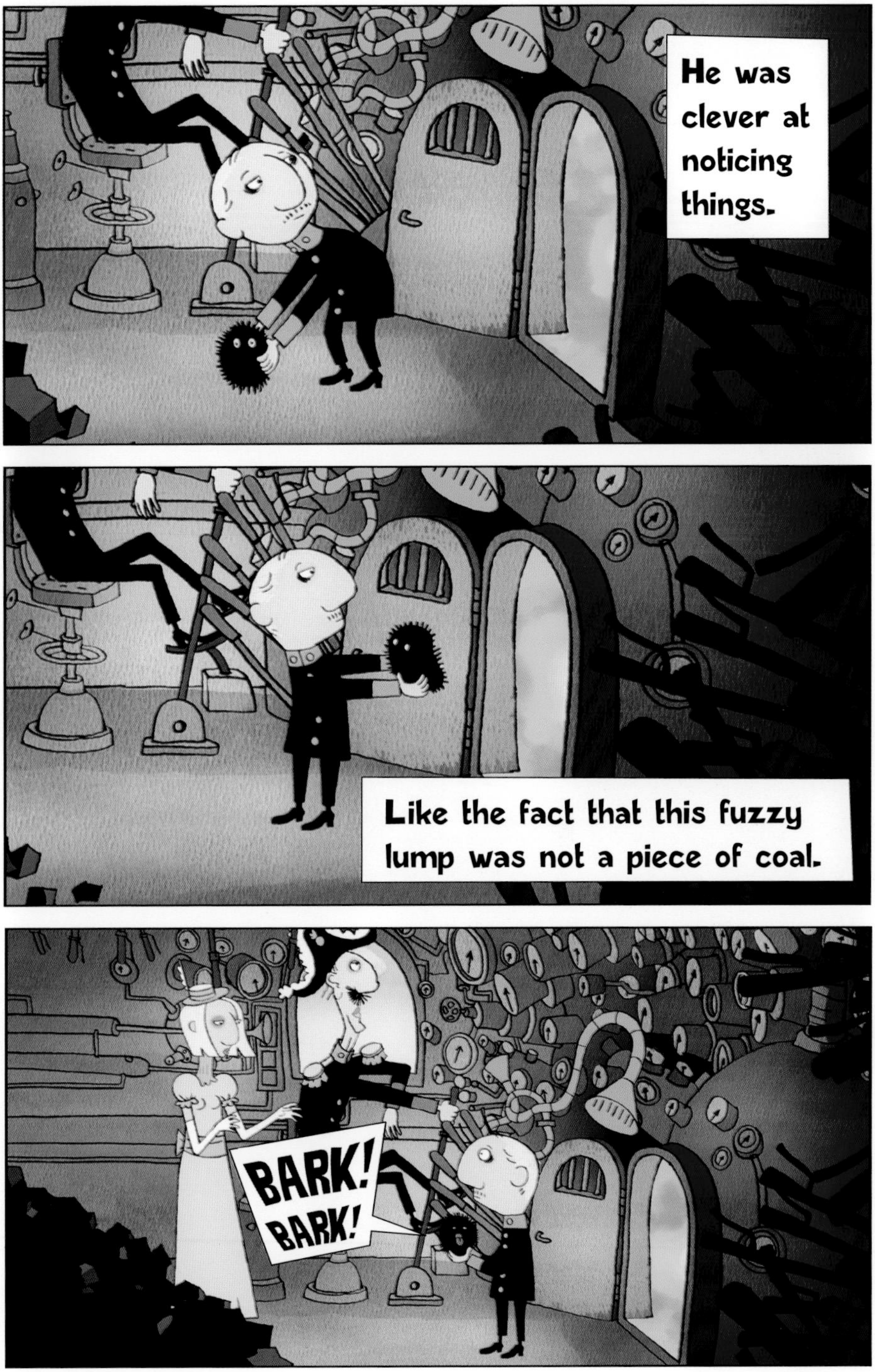
He was clever at noticing things.
Like the fact that this fuzzy lump was not a piece of coal.
BARK! BARK!

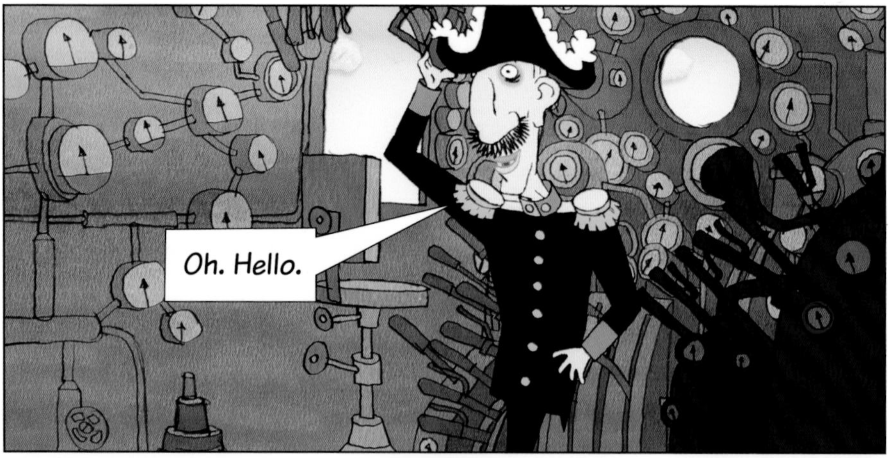
Oh. Hello.

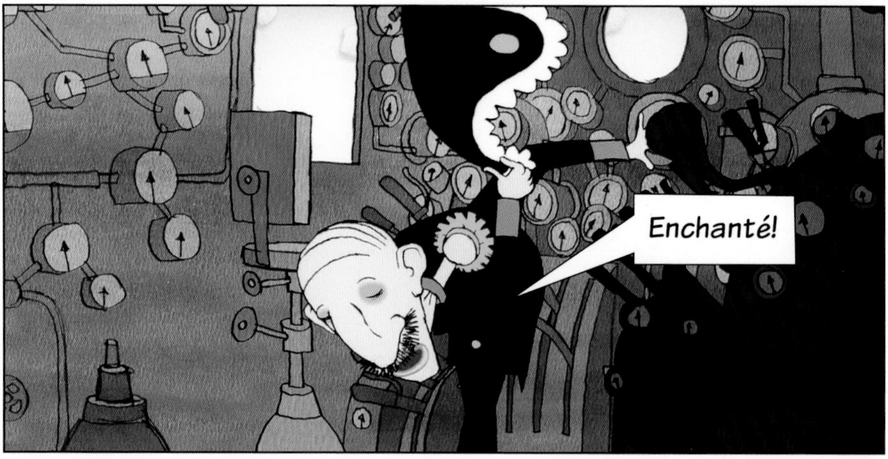
Enchanté!

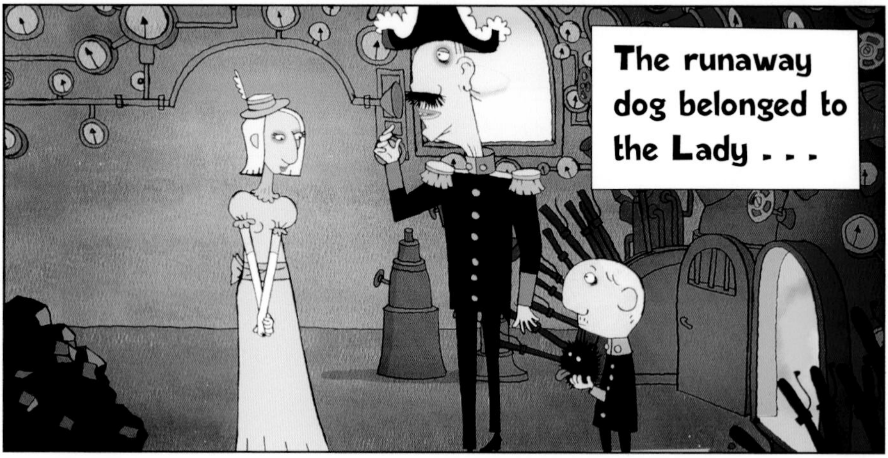
The runaway dog belonged to the Lady . . .

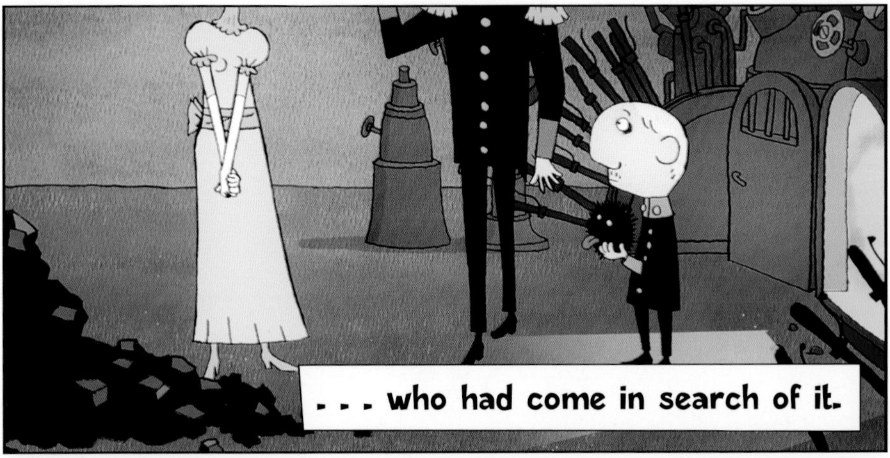
. . . who had come in search of it.

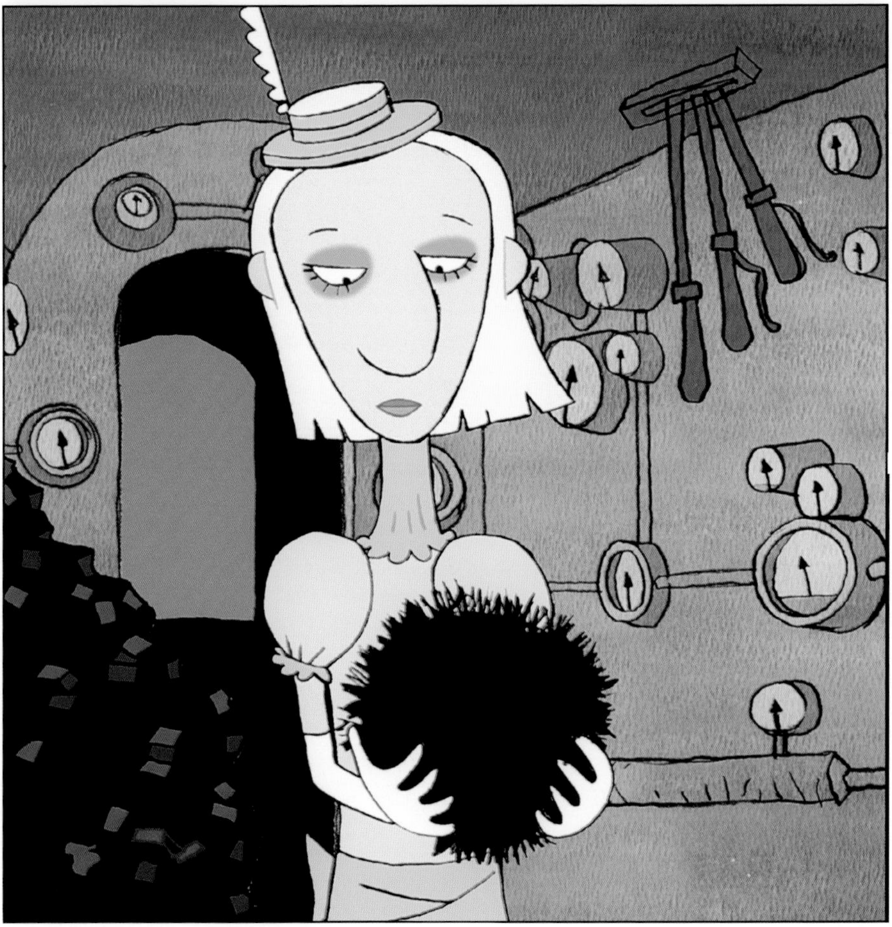

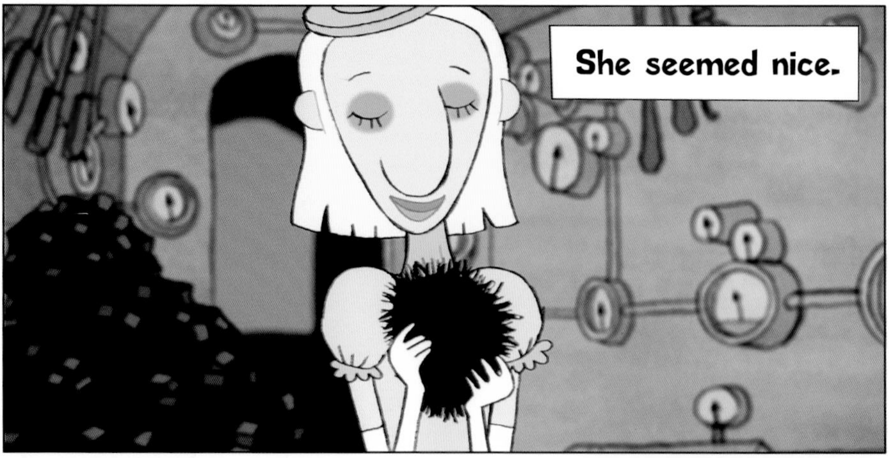
She seemed nice.

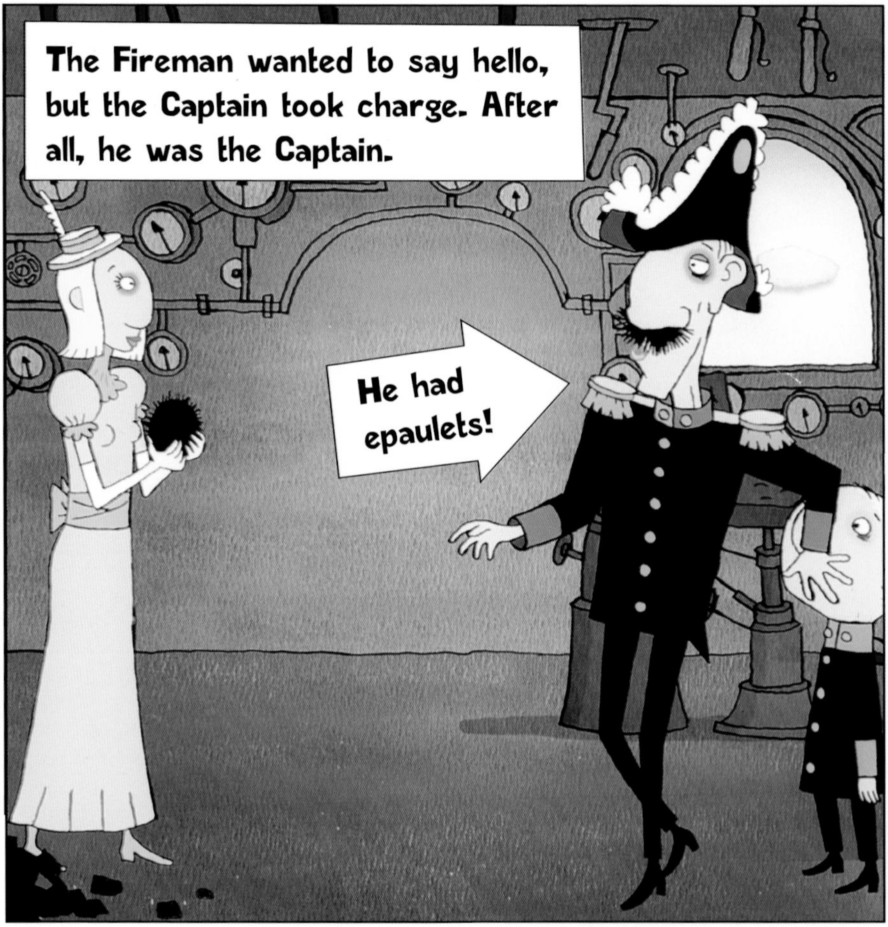
The Fireman wanted to say hello, but the Captain took charge. After all, he was the Captain.
He had epaulets!

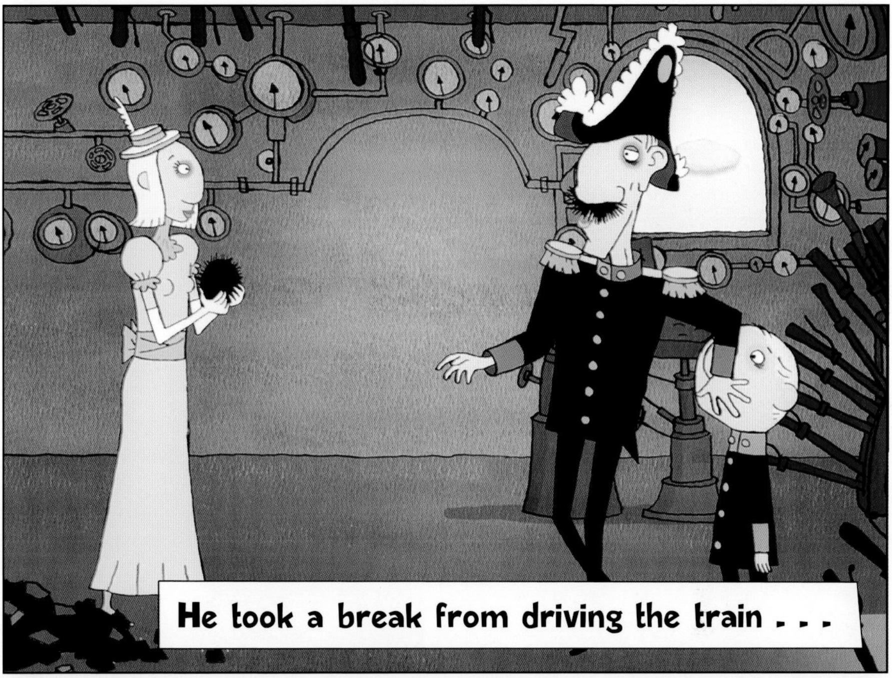
He took a break from driving the train . . .

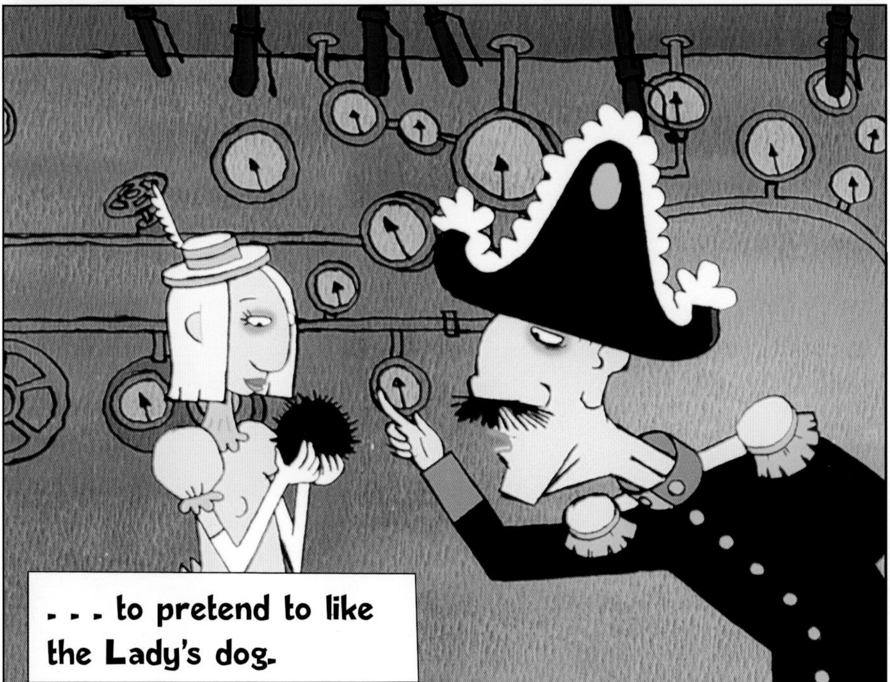
. . . to pretend to like
the Lady's dog.

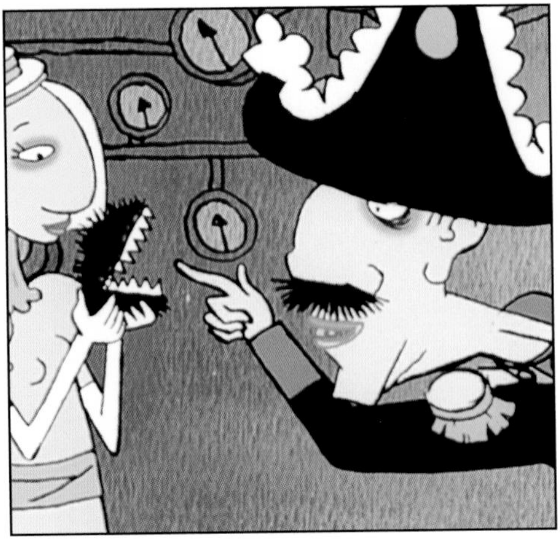

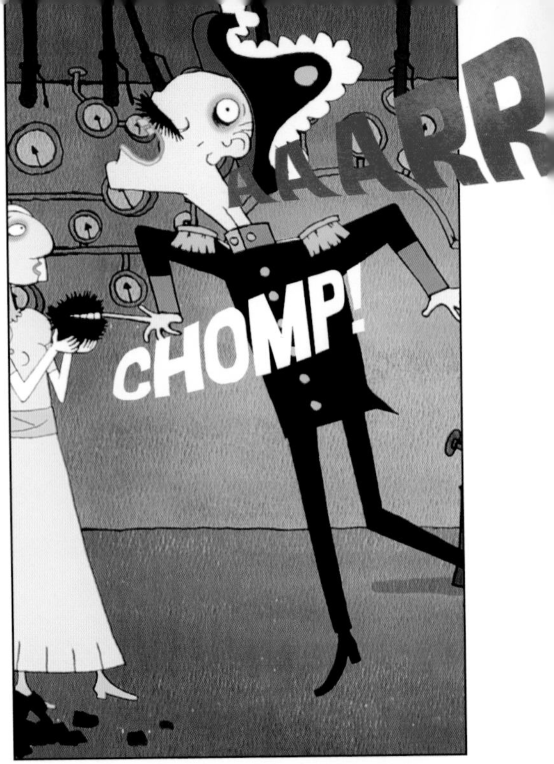
AAARR
CHOMP!

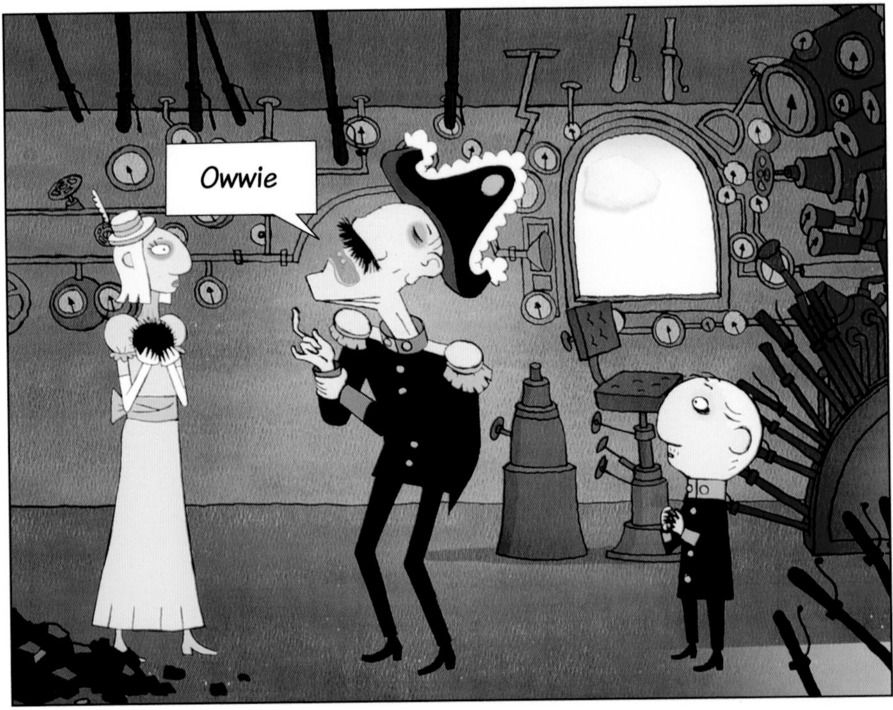
Owwie

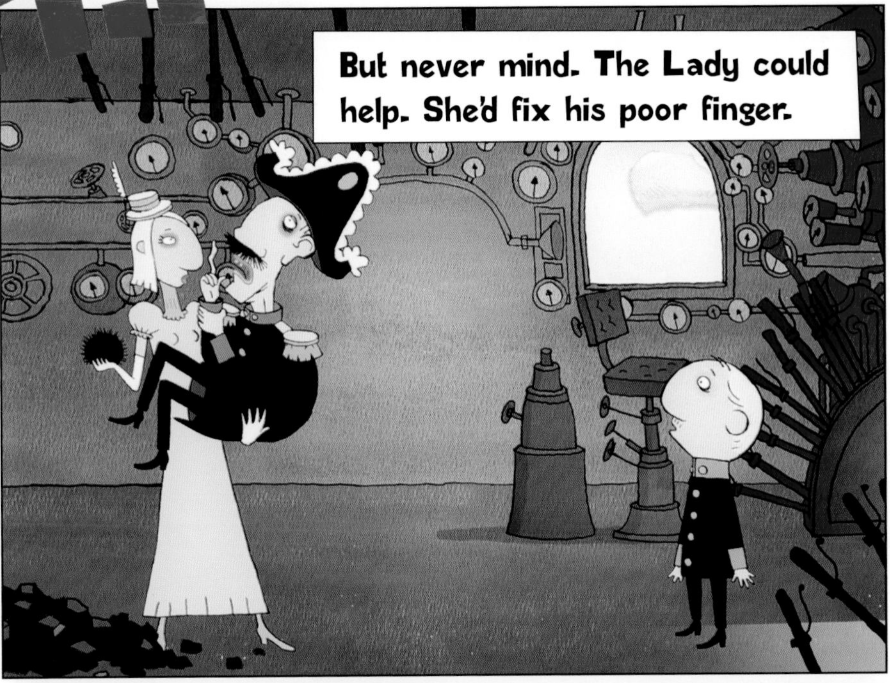
But never mind. The Lady could help. She'd fix his poor finger.

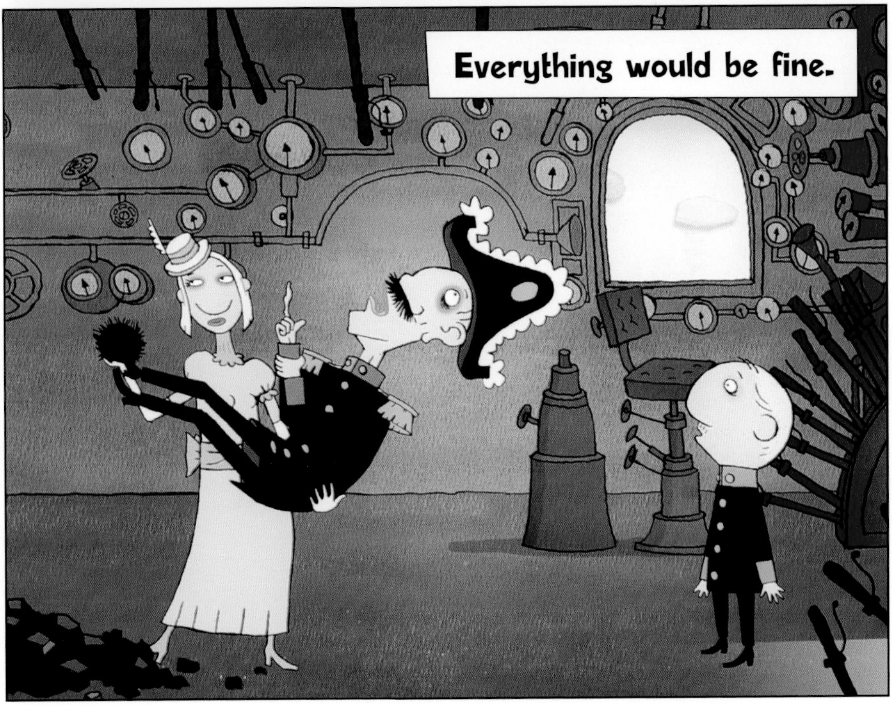
Everything would be fine.

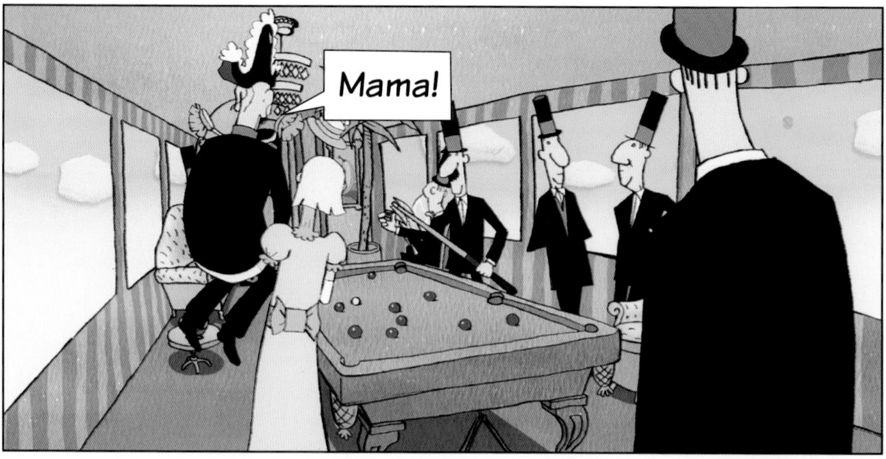
Mama!

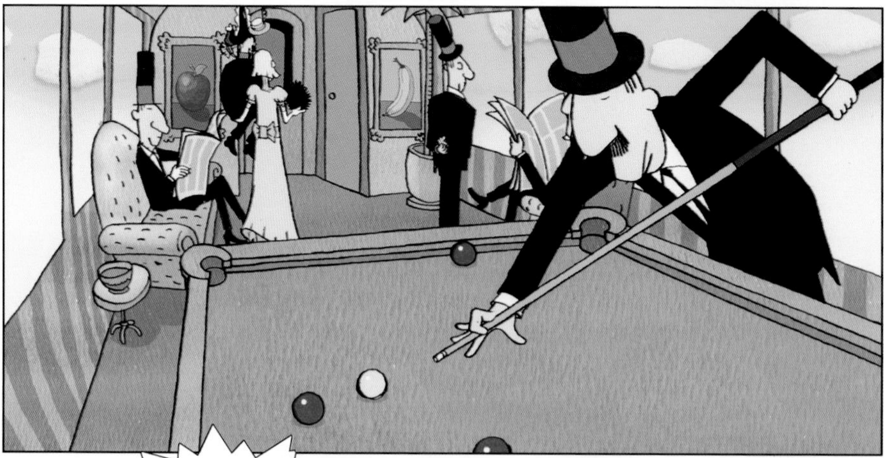

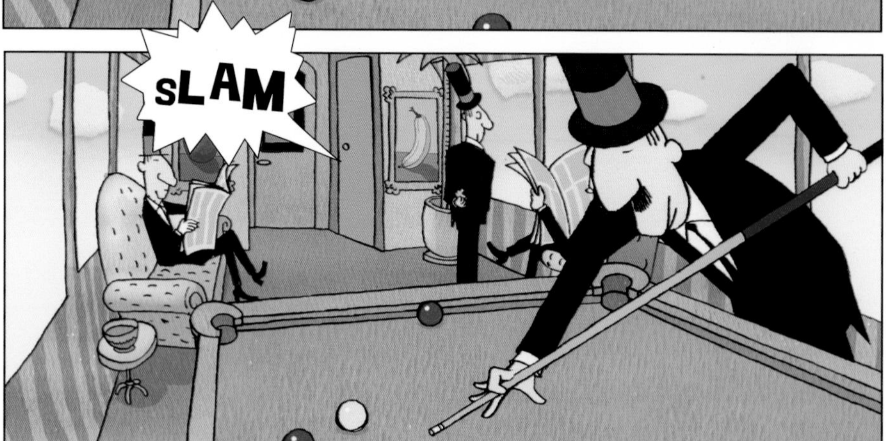
SLAM

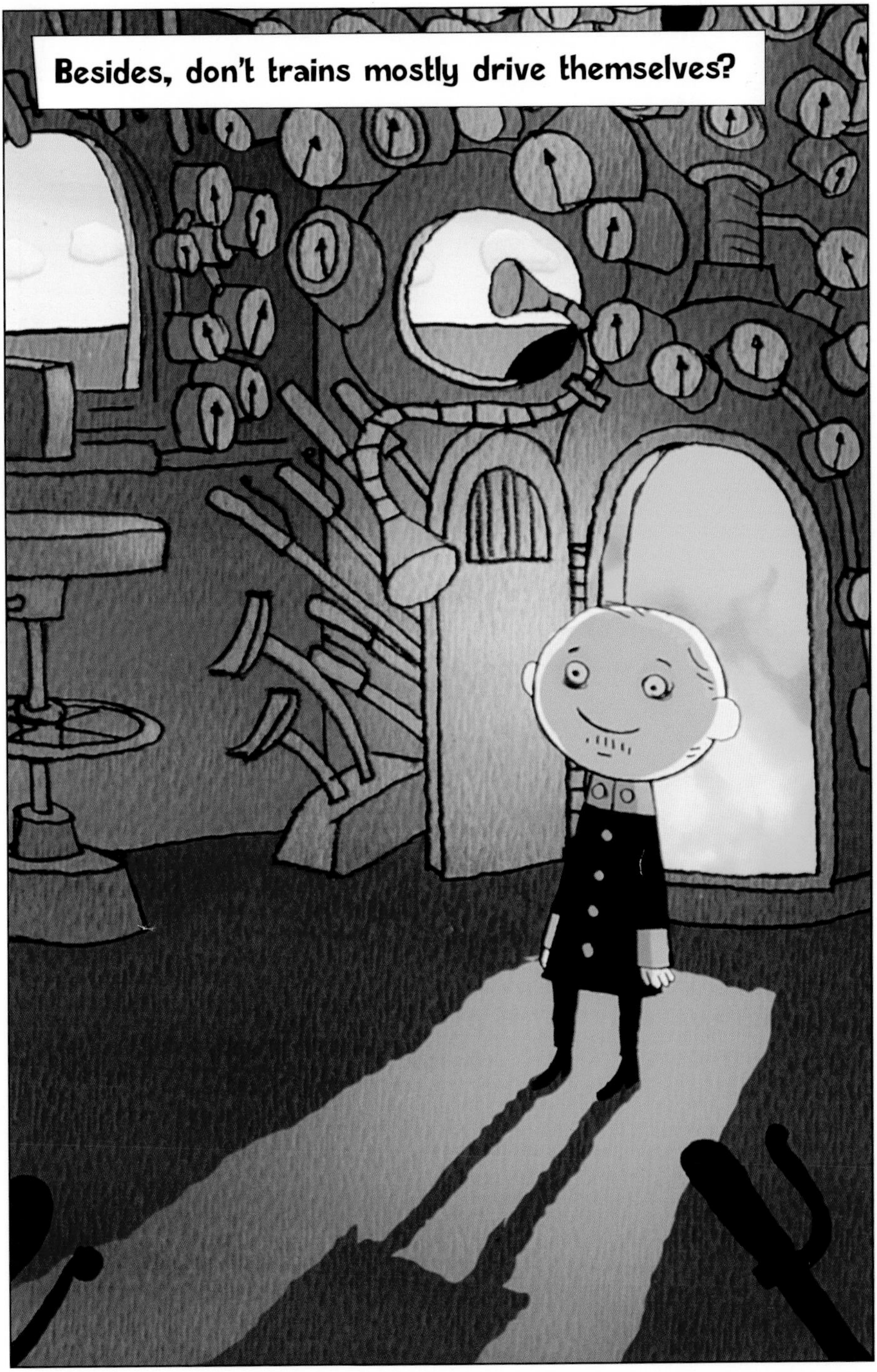
Besides, don't trains mostly drive themselves?

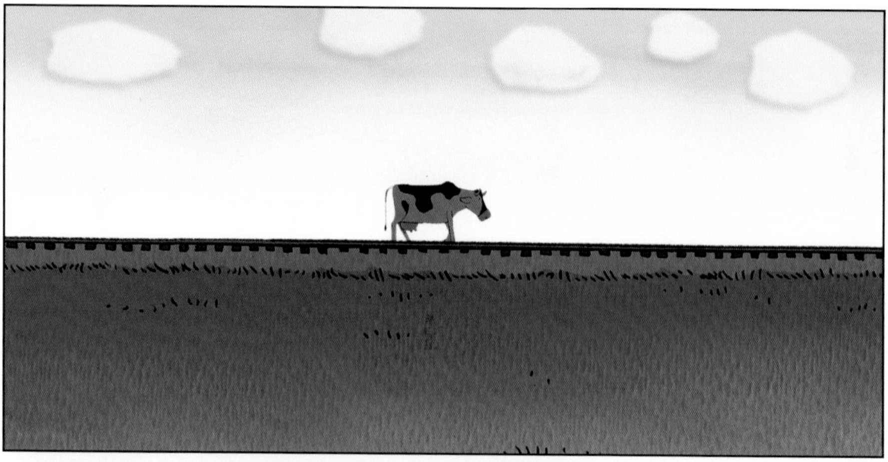

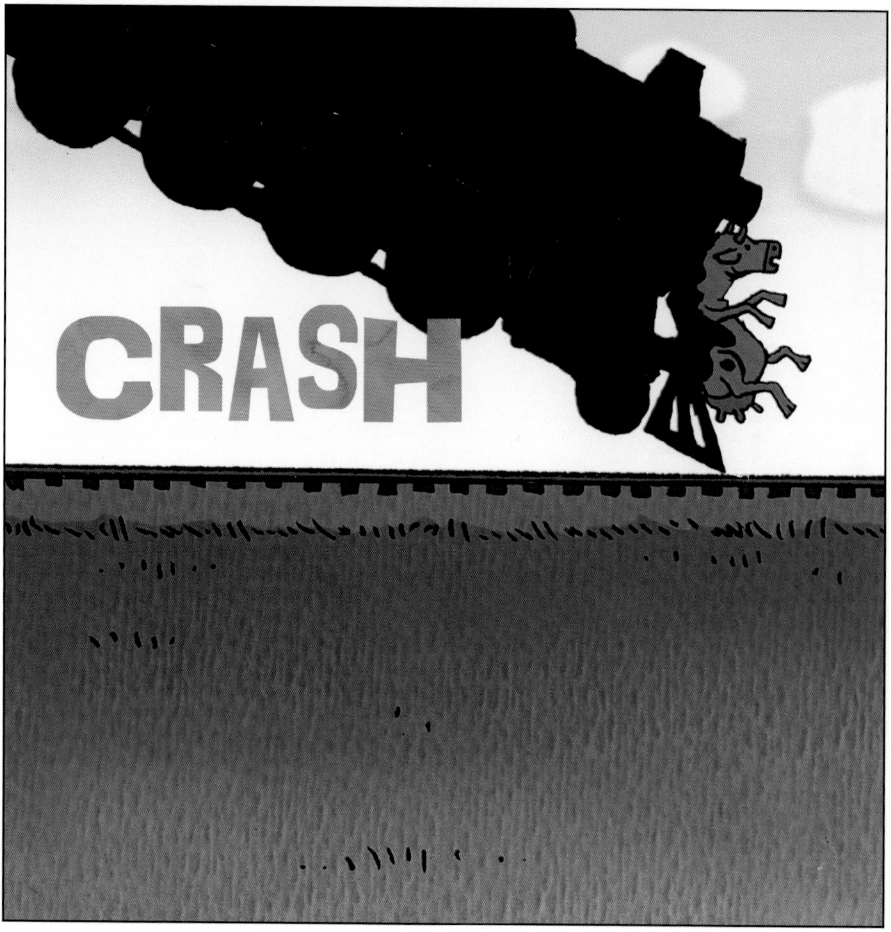
CRASH

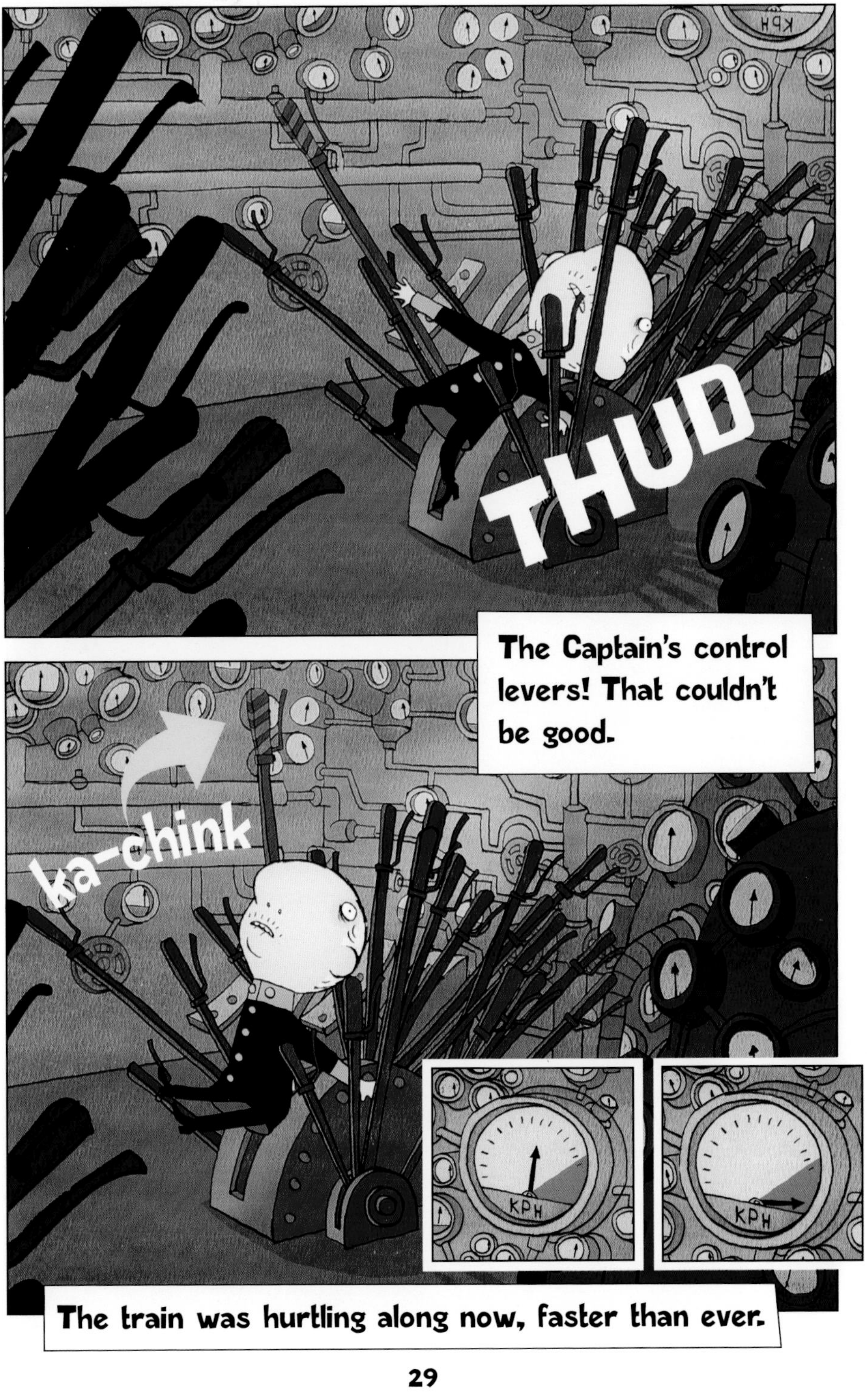
THUD
The Captain's control levers! That couldn't be good.
ka-chink
KPH
KPH
The train was hurtling along now, faster than ever.

Captain?

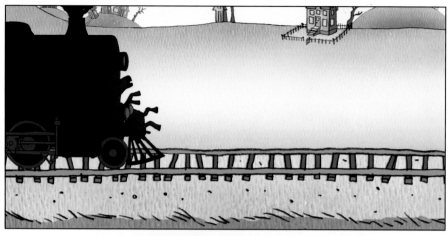

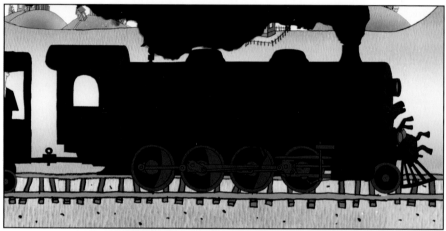

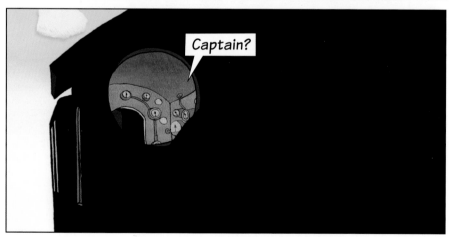

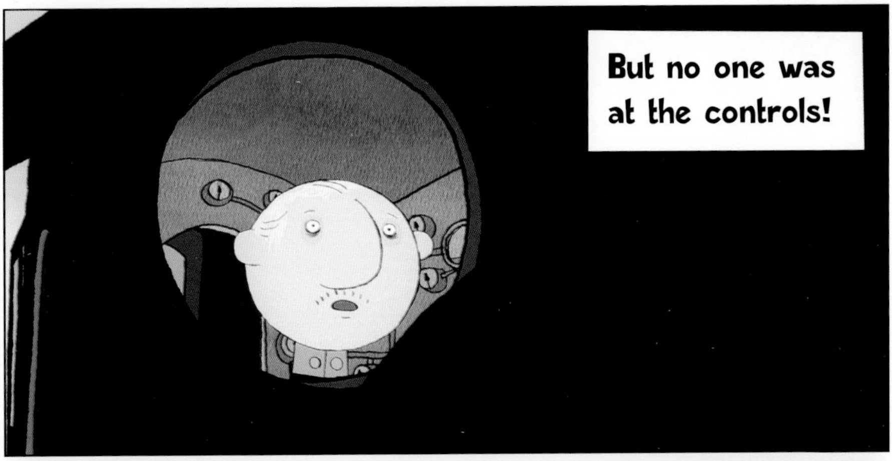
But no one was at the controls!

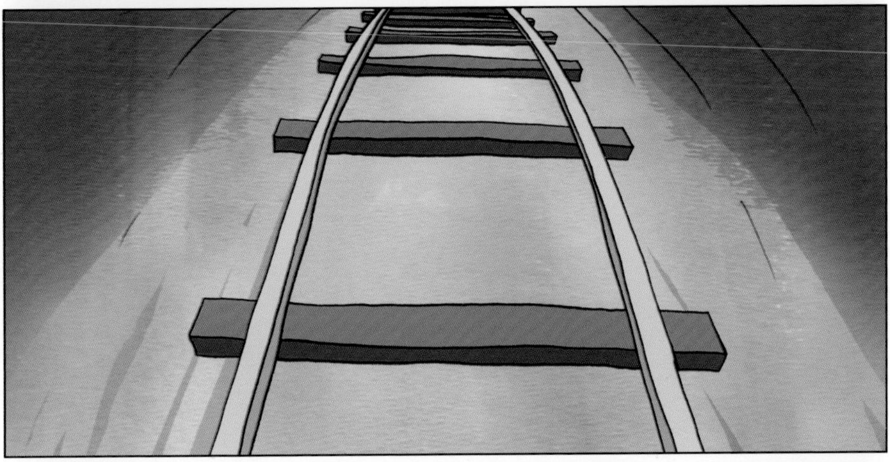

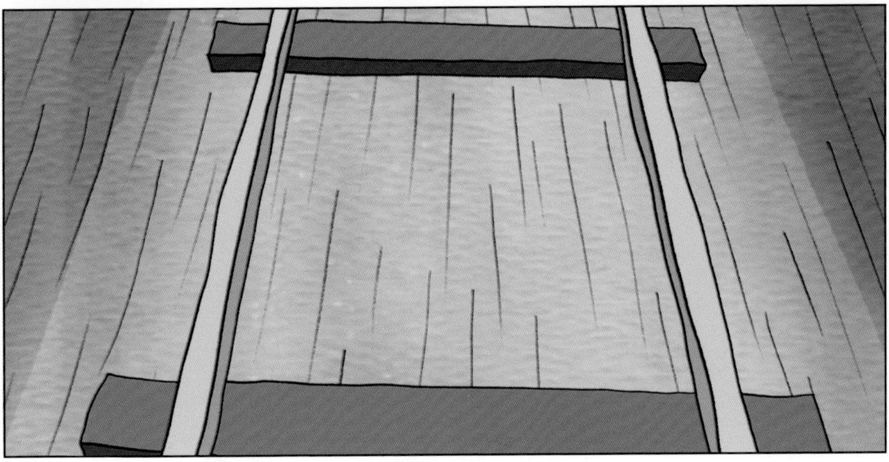

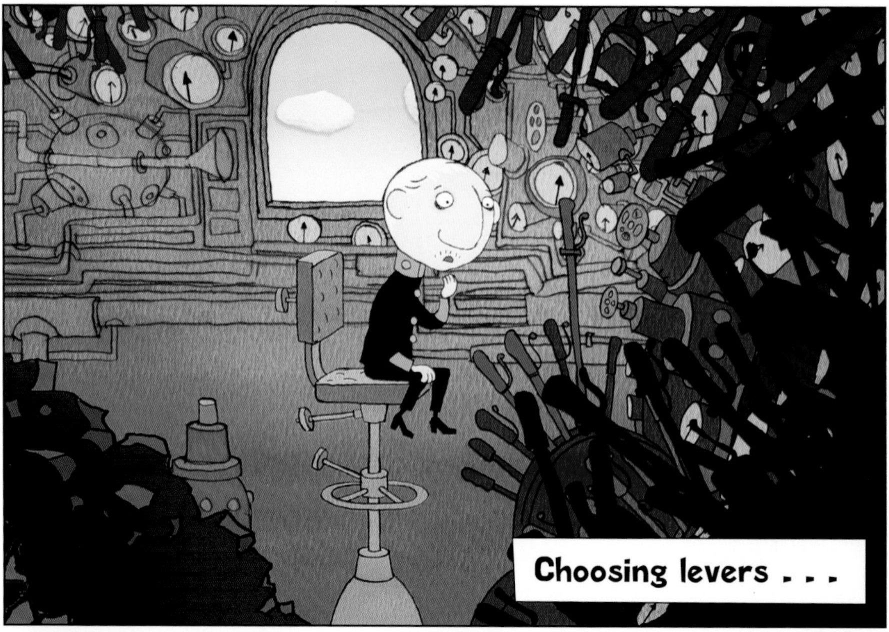
Choosing levers . . .

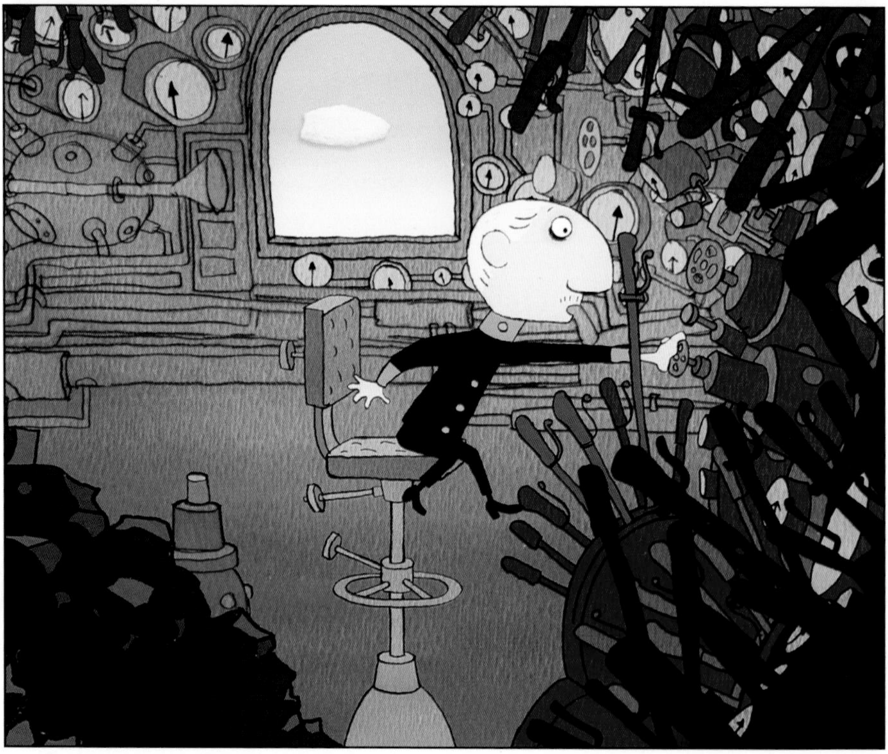

. . . was not something the Fireman was clever at.

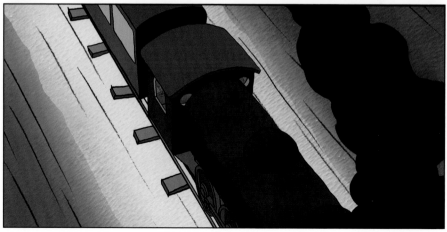

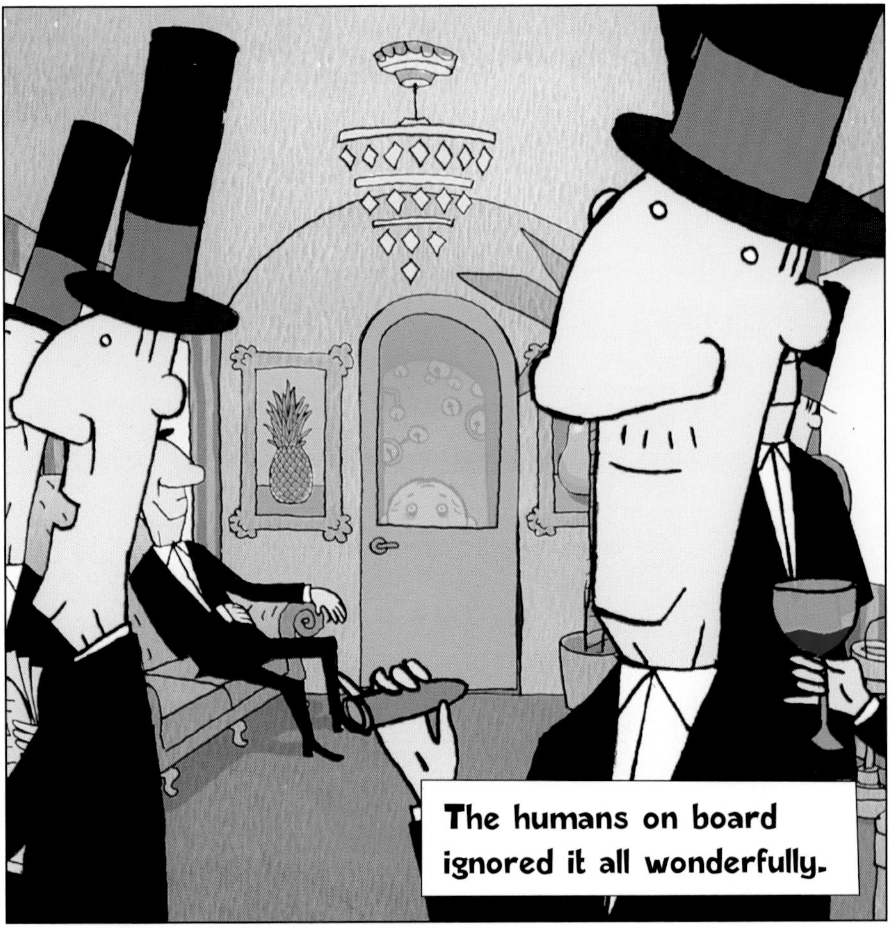
The humans on board
ignored it all wonderfully.

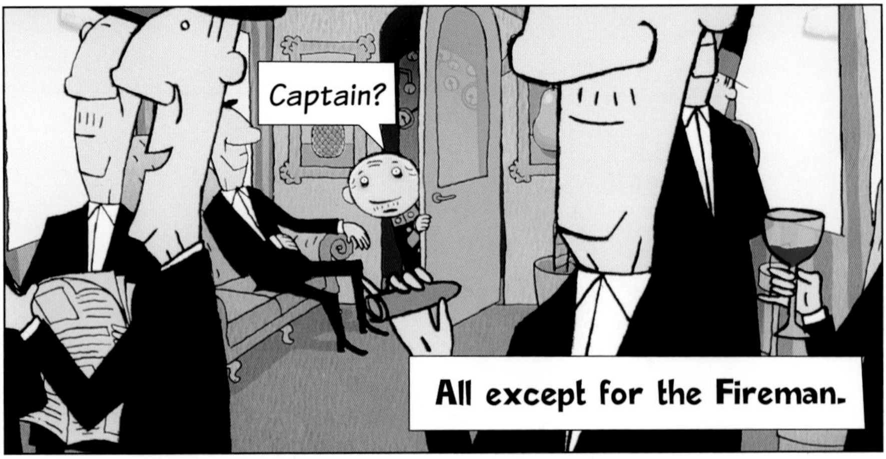
Captain?
All except for the Fireman.

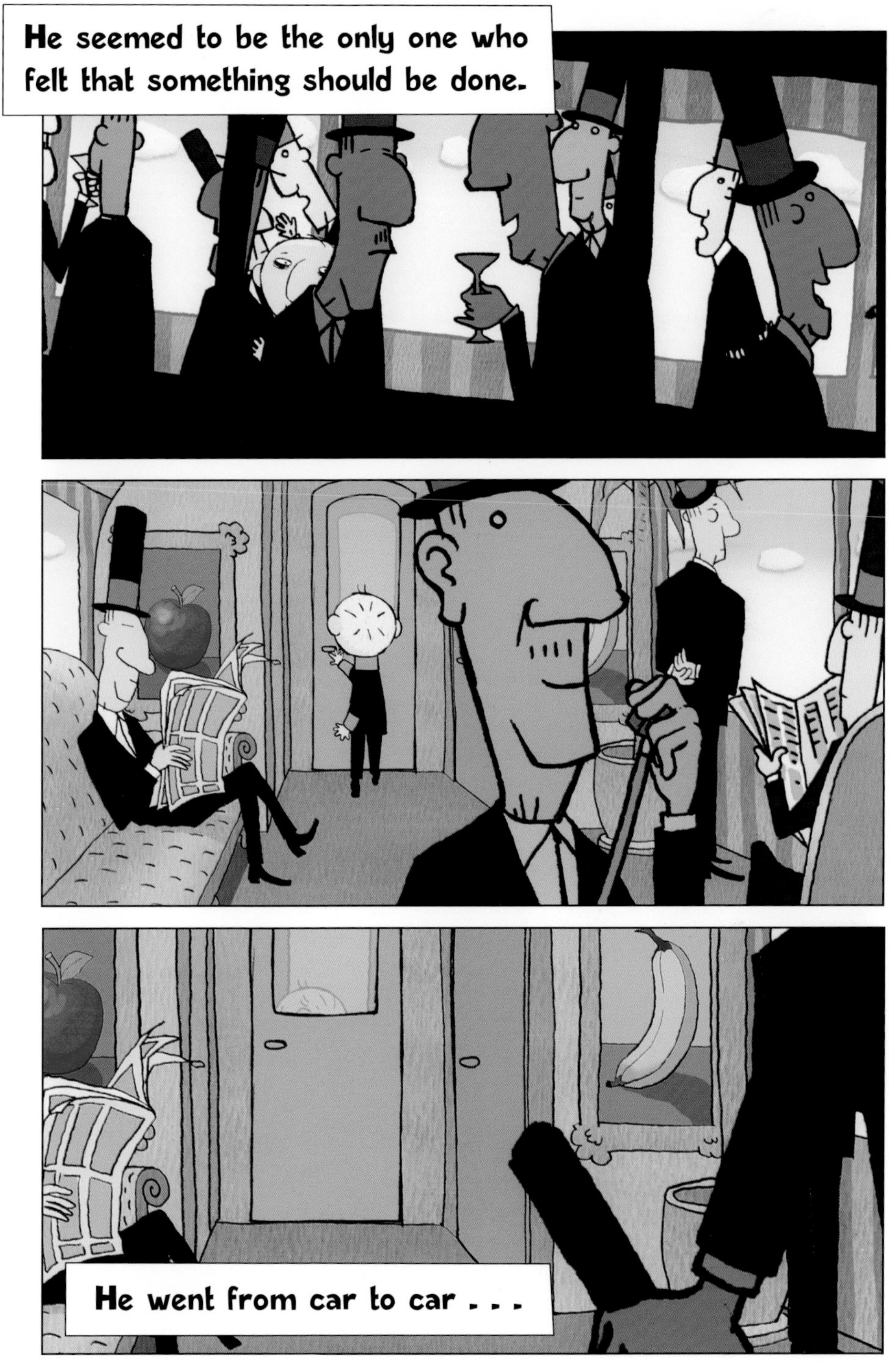
He seemed to be the only one who felt that something should be done.
He went from car to car . . .

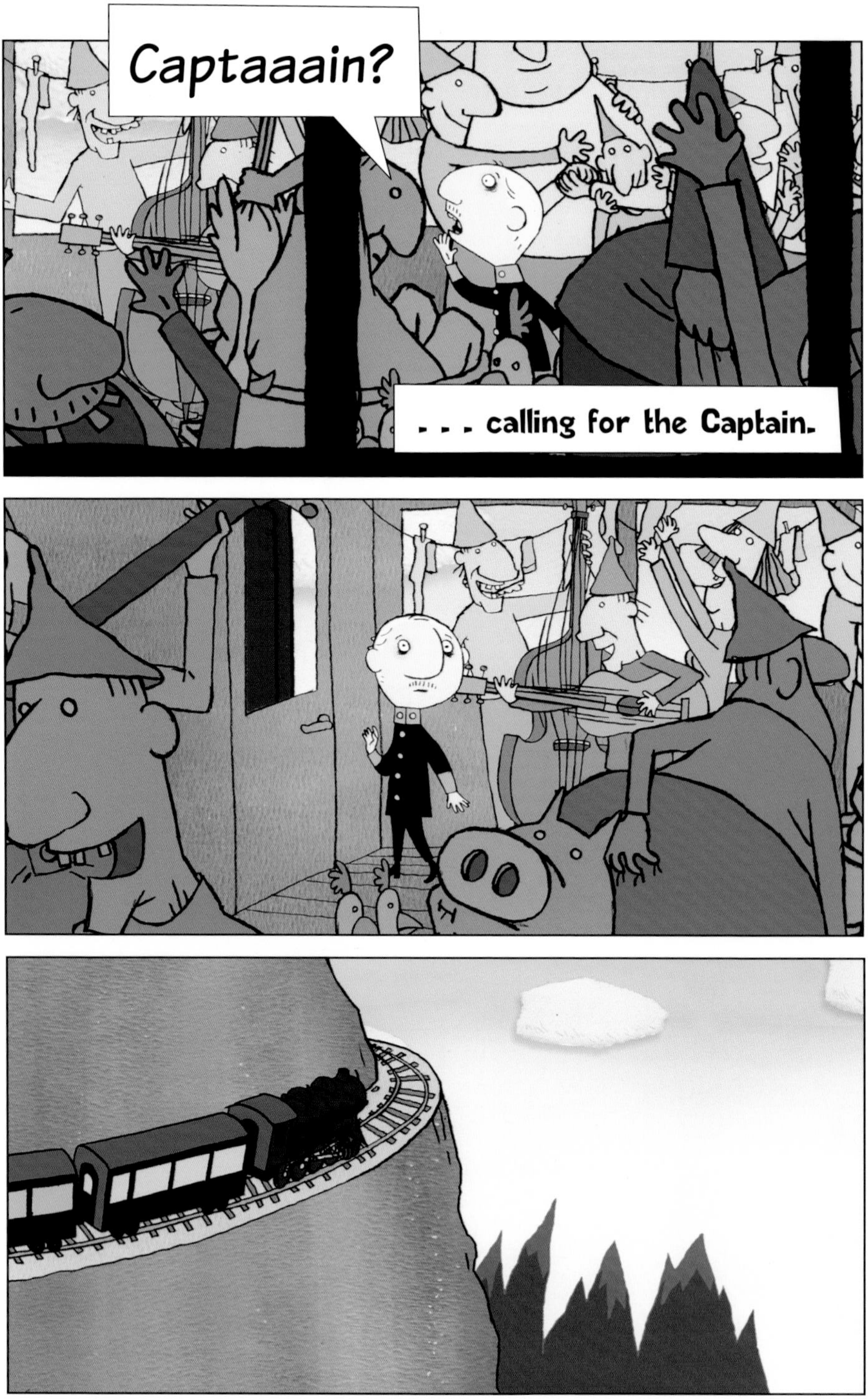
Captaaaain?
. . . calling for the Captain.

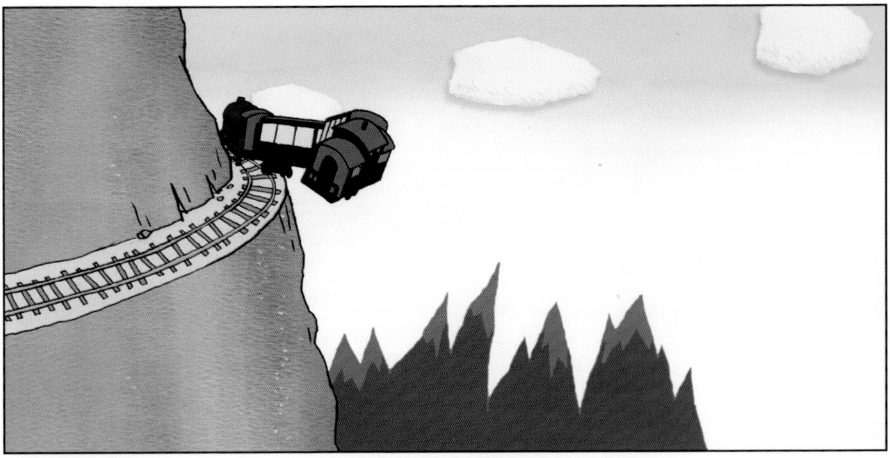

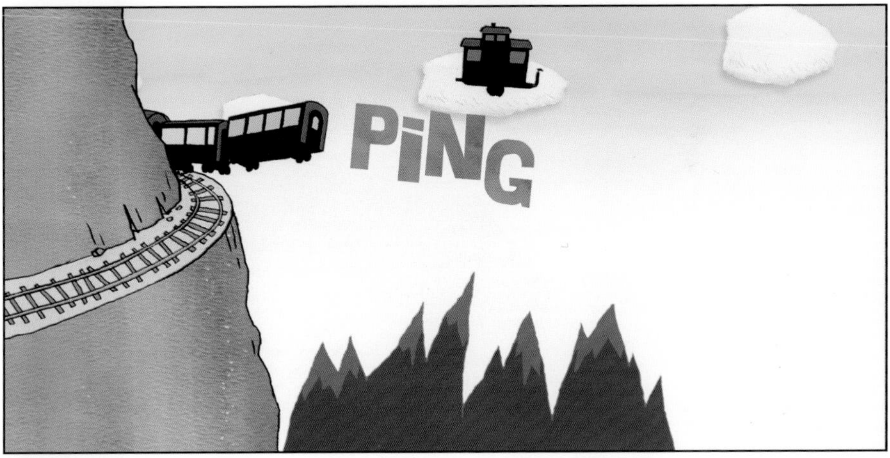
PiNG

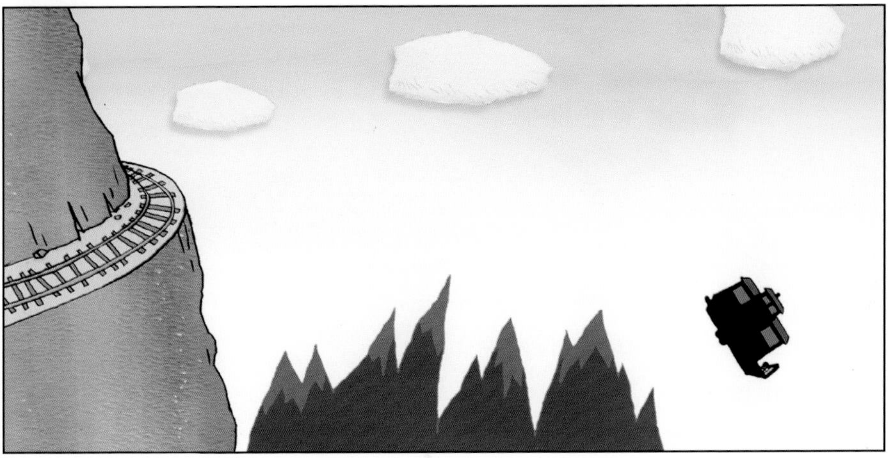

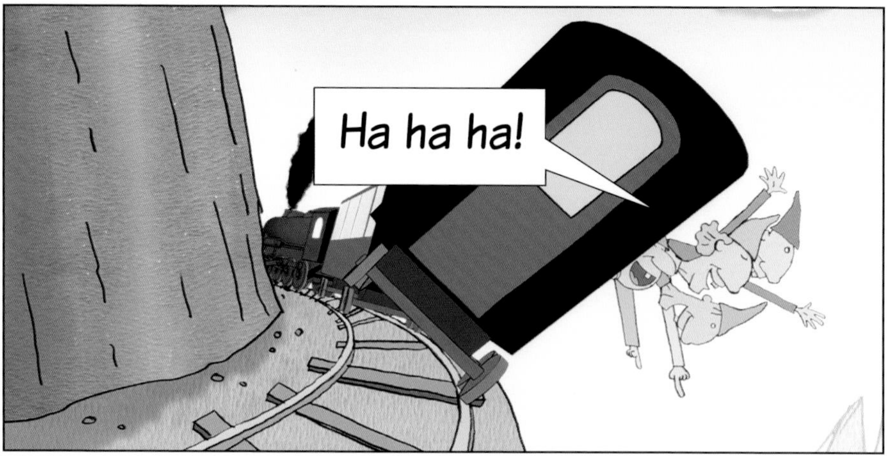
Ha ha ha!

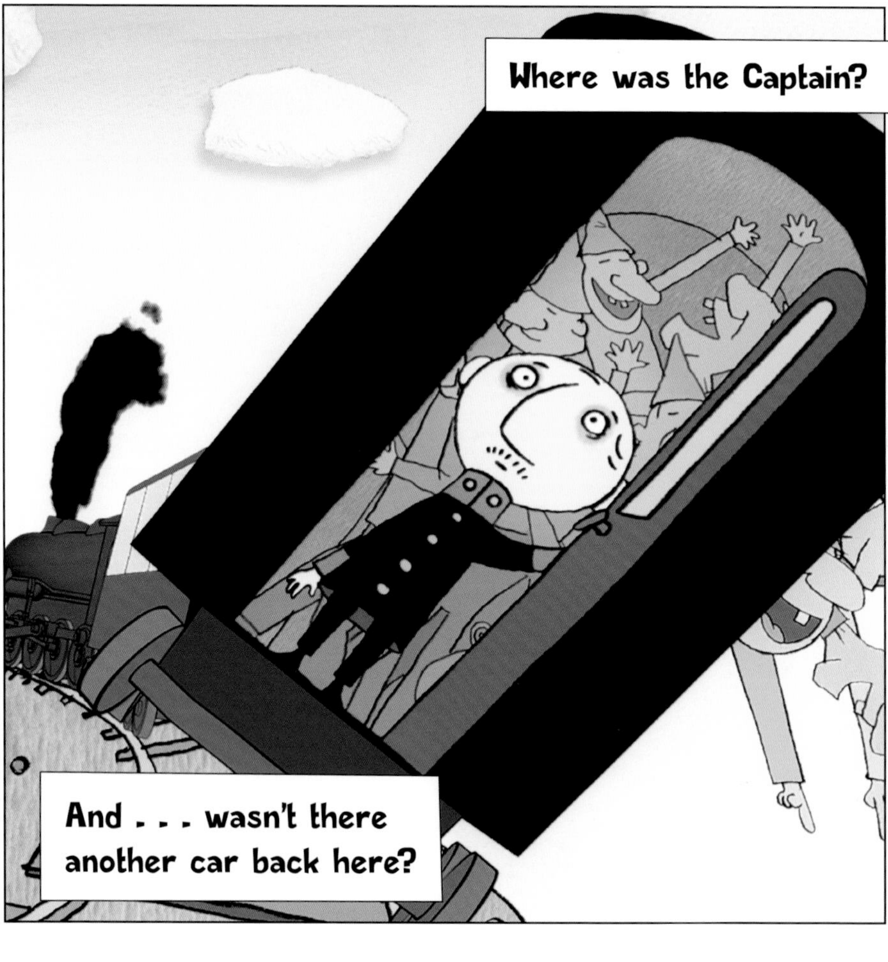
Where was the Captain?
And . . . wasn't there another car back here?

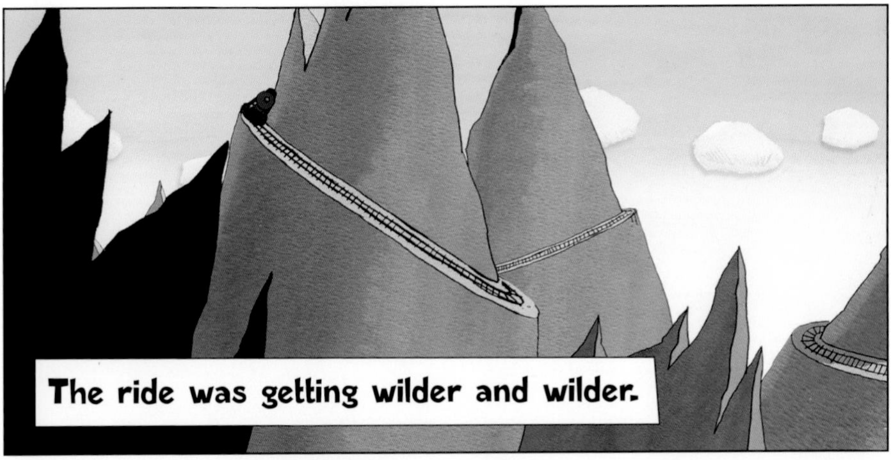
The ride was getting wilder and wilder.

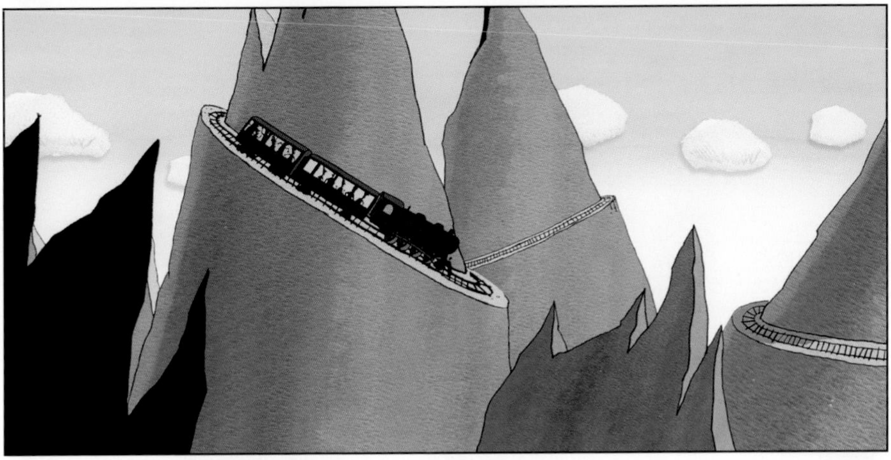

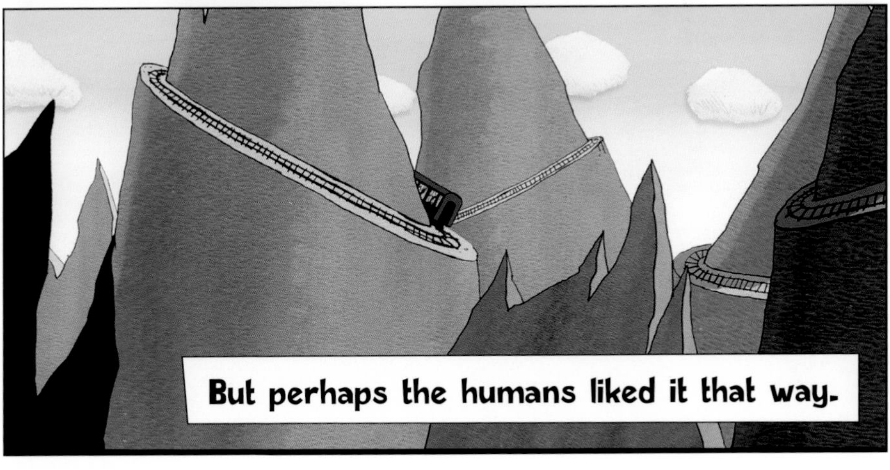
But perhaps the humans liked it that way.

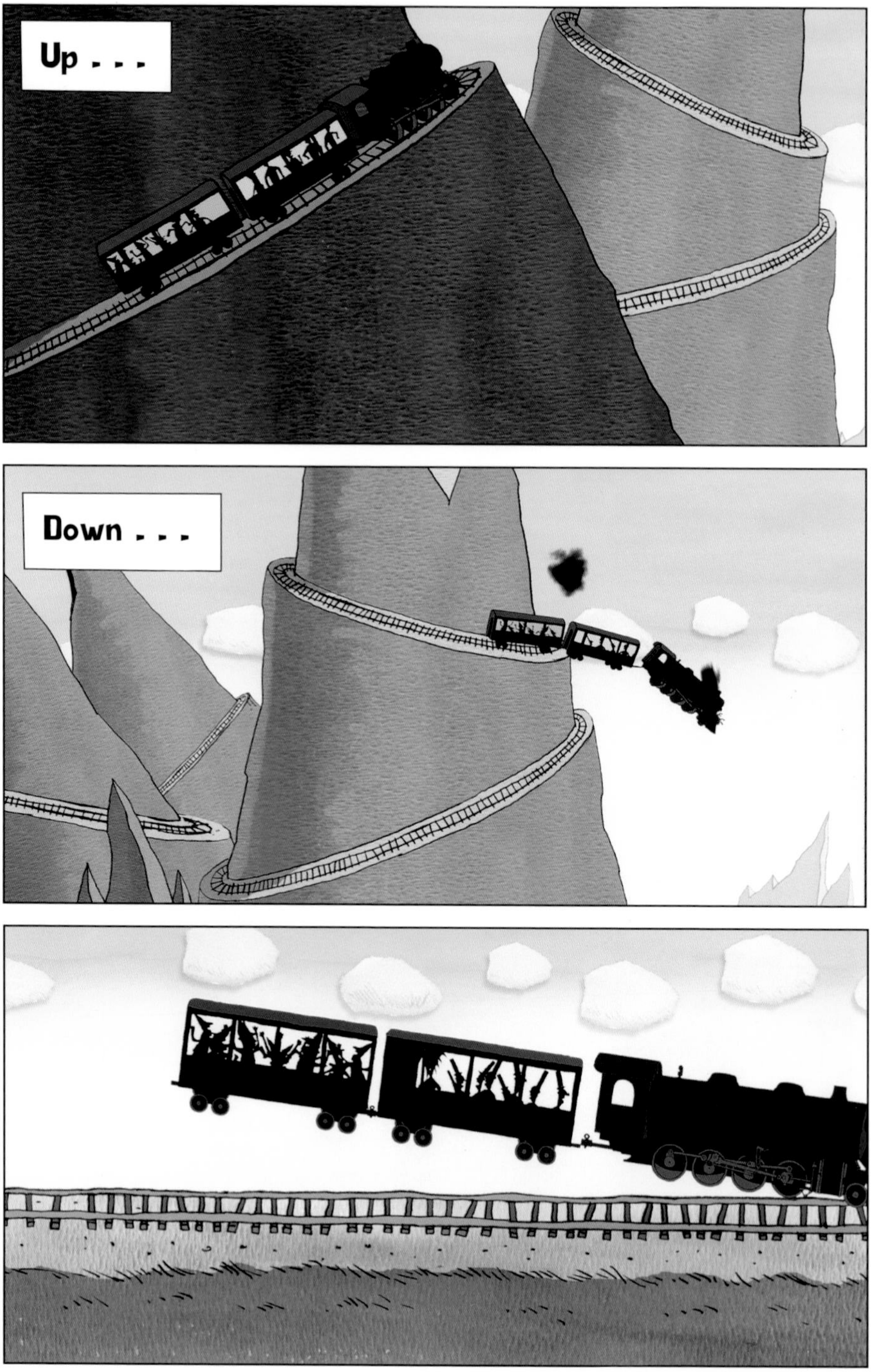
Up . . .
Down . . .

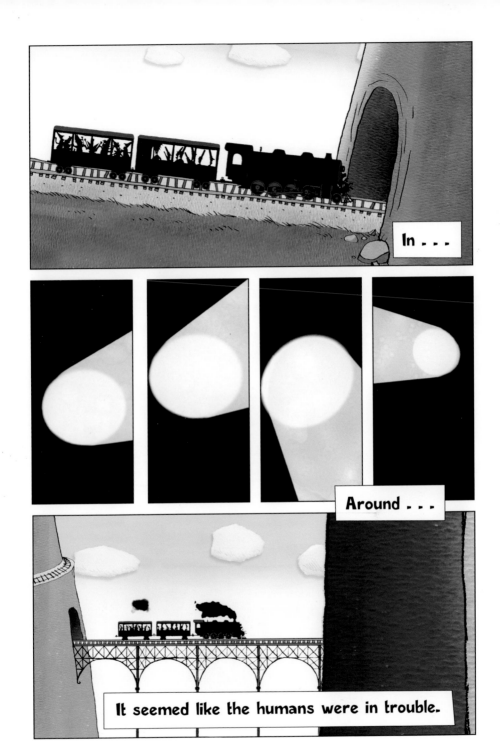

In . . .

Around . . .

It seemed like the humans were in trouble.

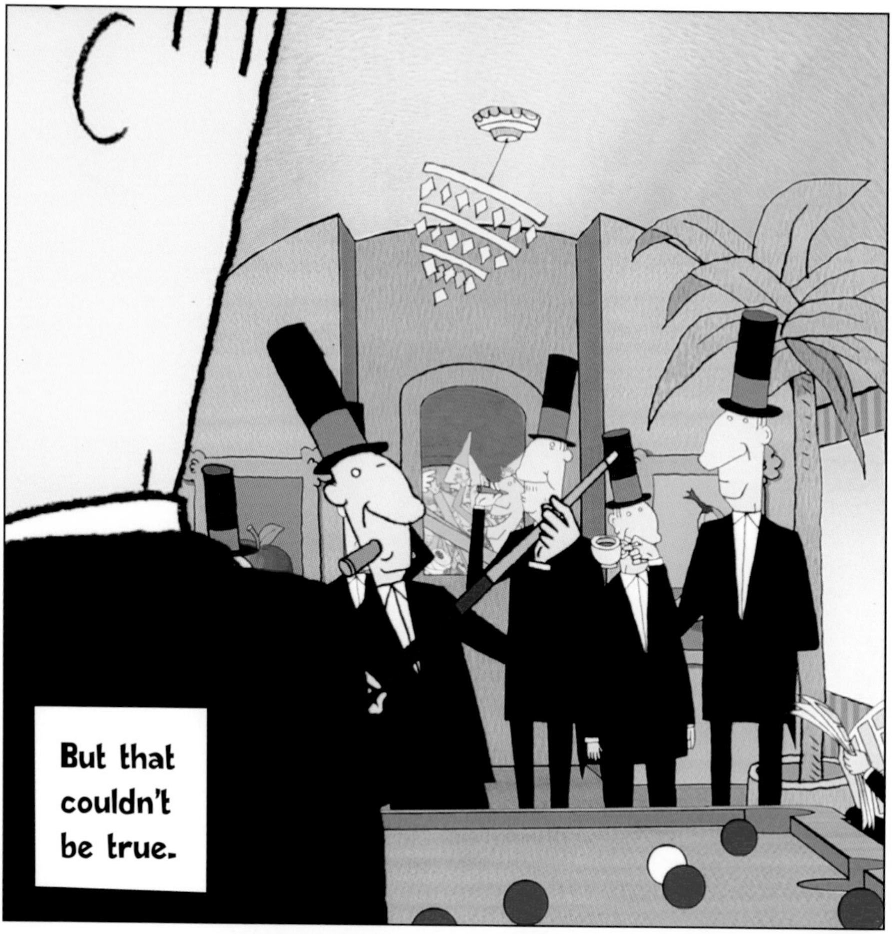
But that
couldn't
be true.

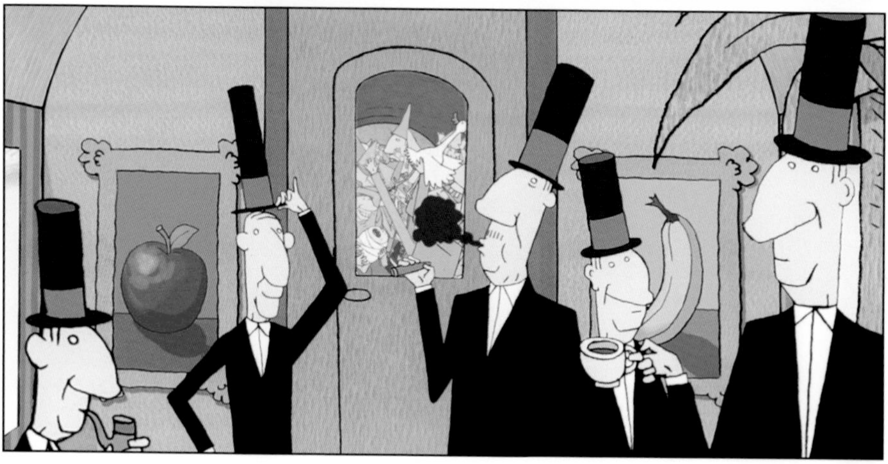

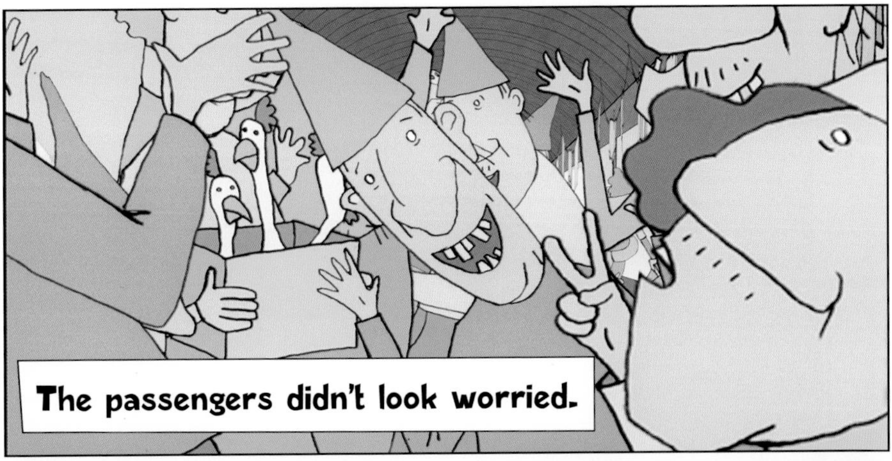
The passengers didn't look worried.

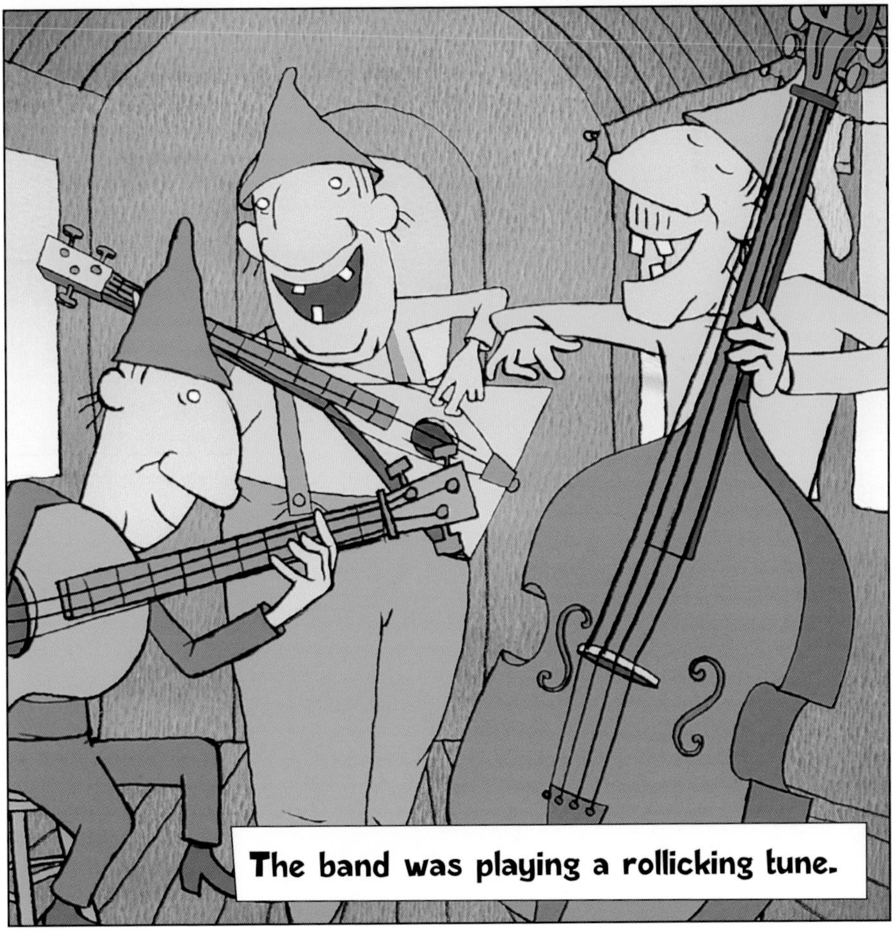
The band was playing a rollicking tune.

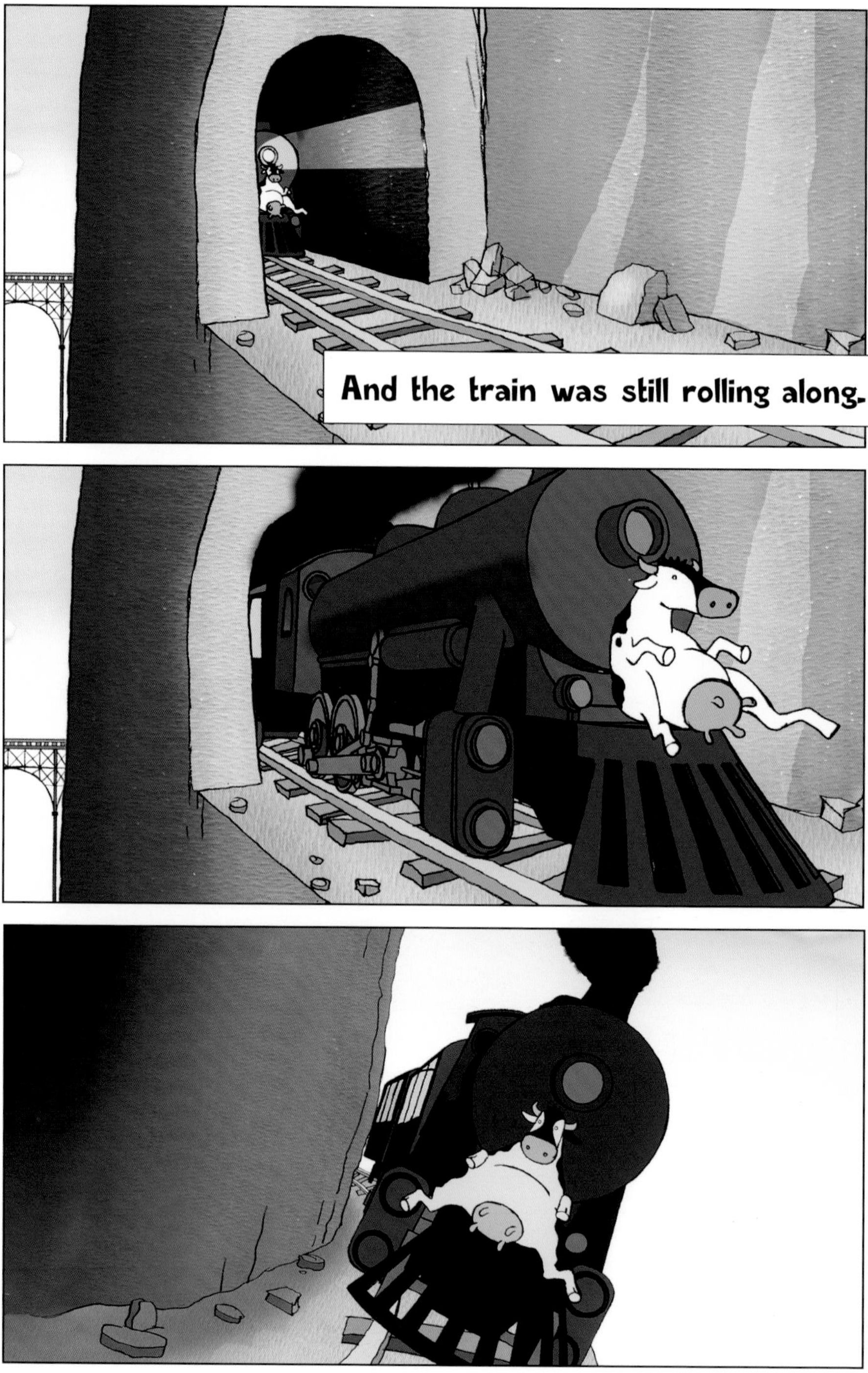
And the train was still rolling along.

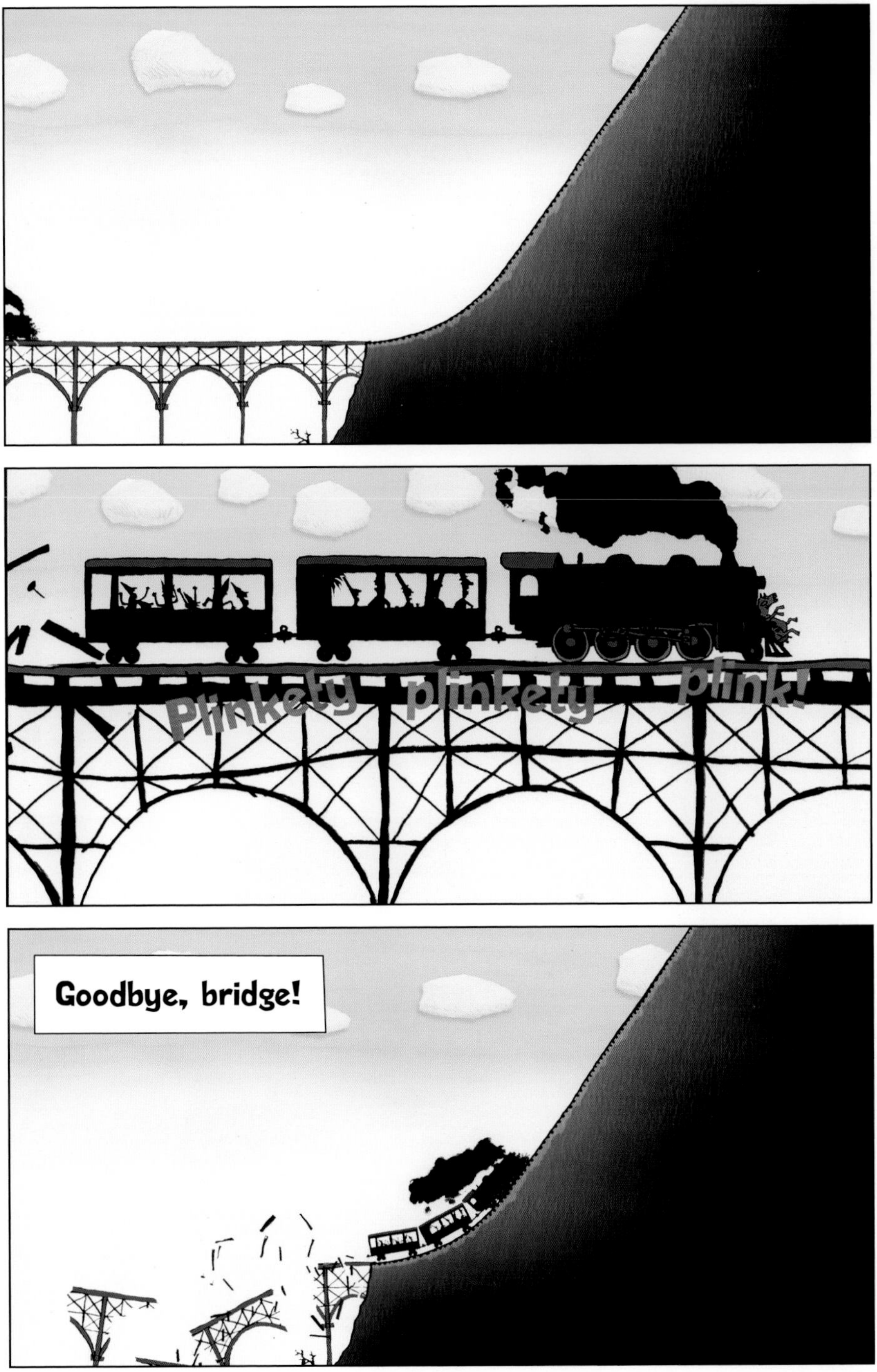
Plinkety plinkety plink!
Goodbye, bridge!

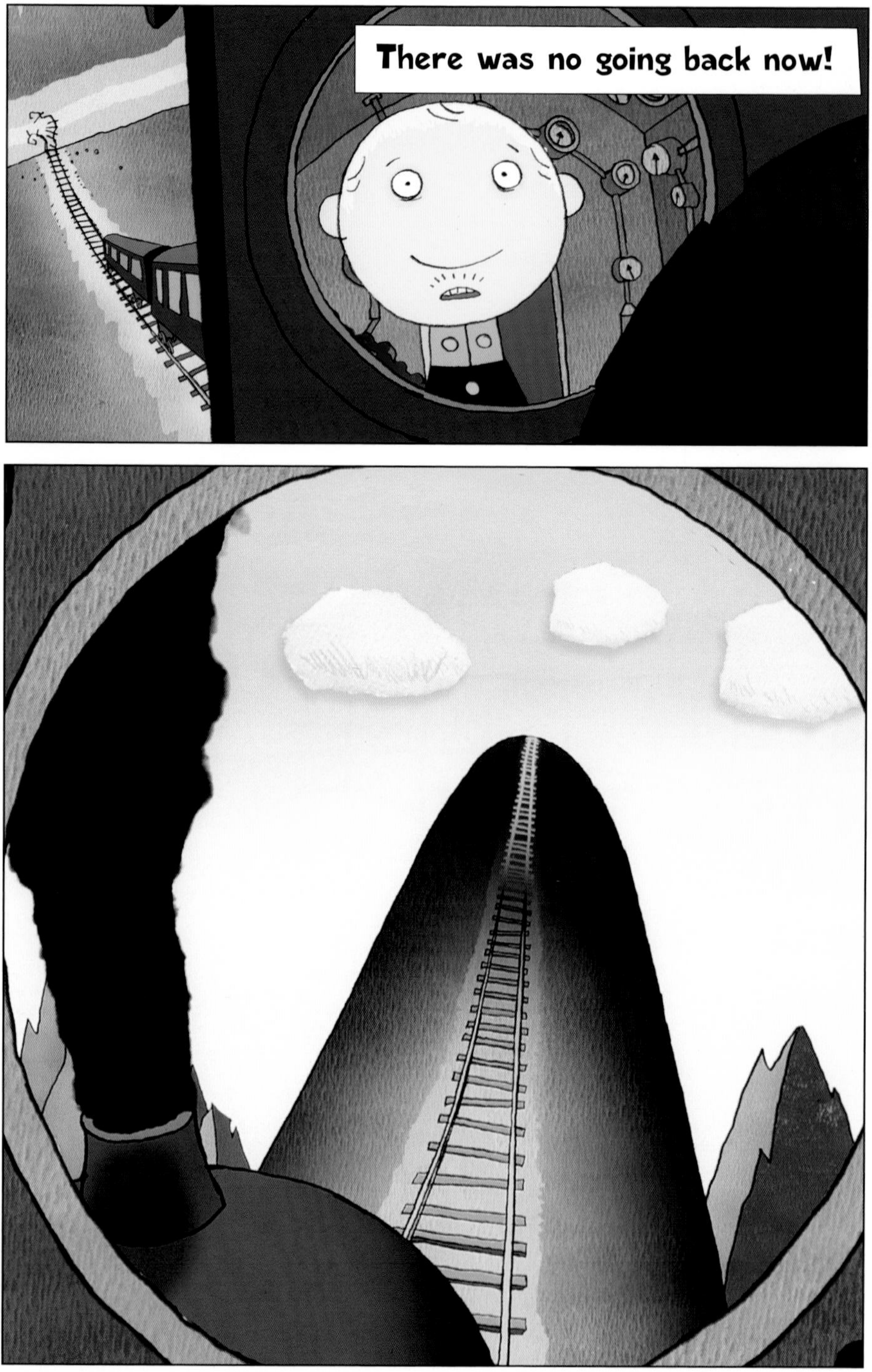
There was no going back now!

The Fireman worked as hard as he could to get the train over the mountain.

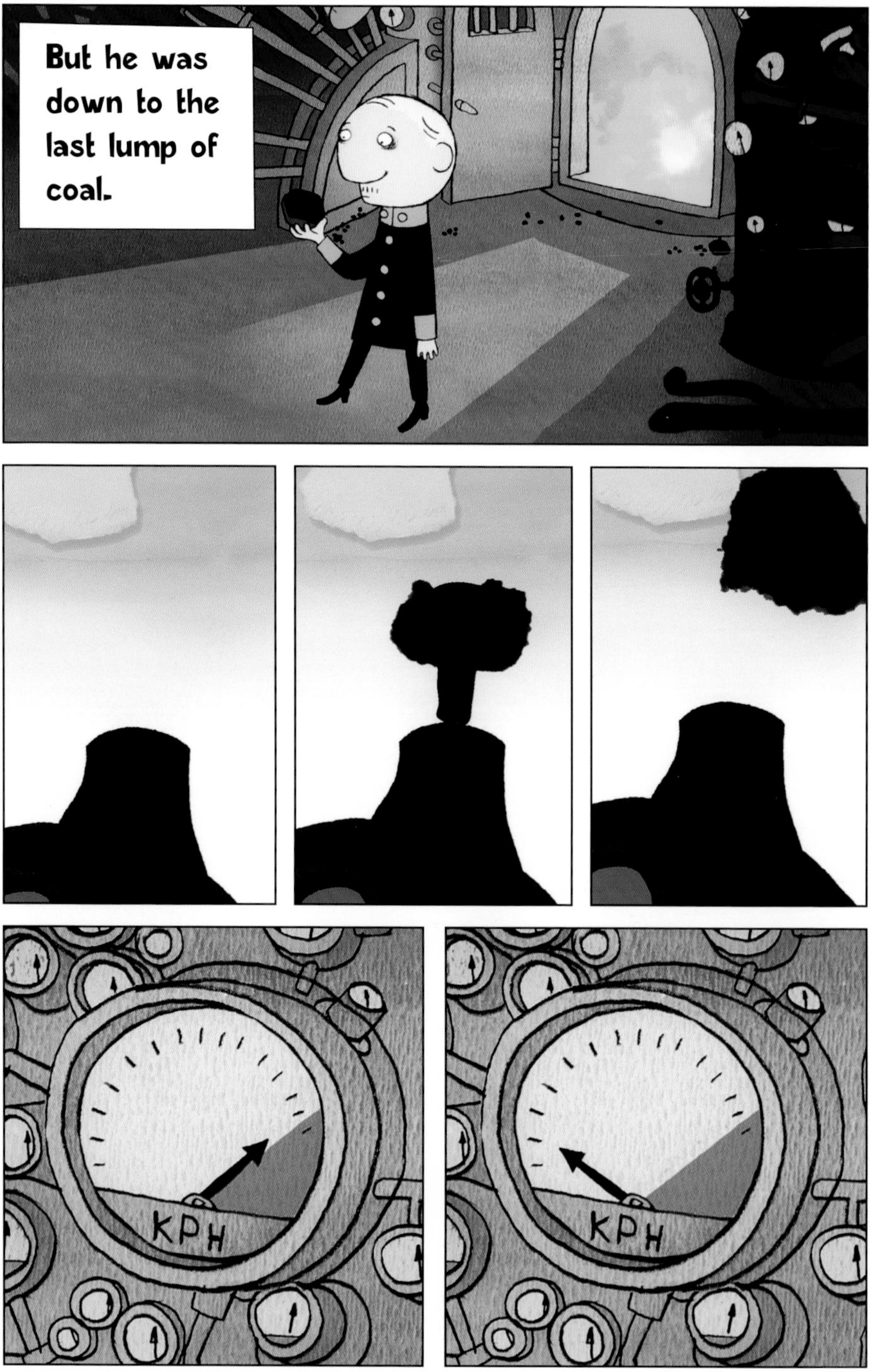
But he was down to the last lump of coal.
KPH
KPH

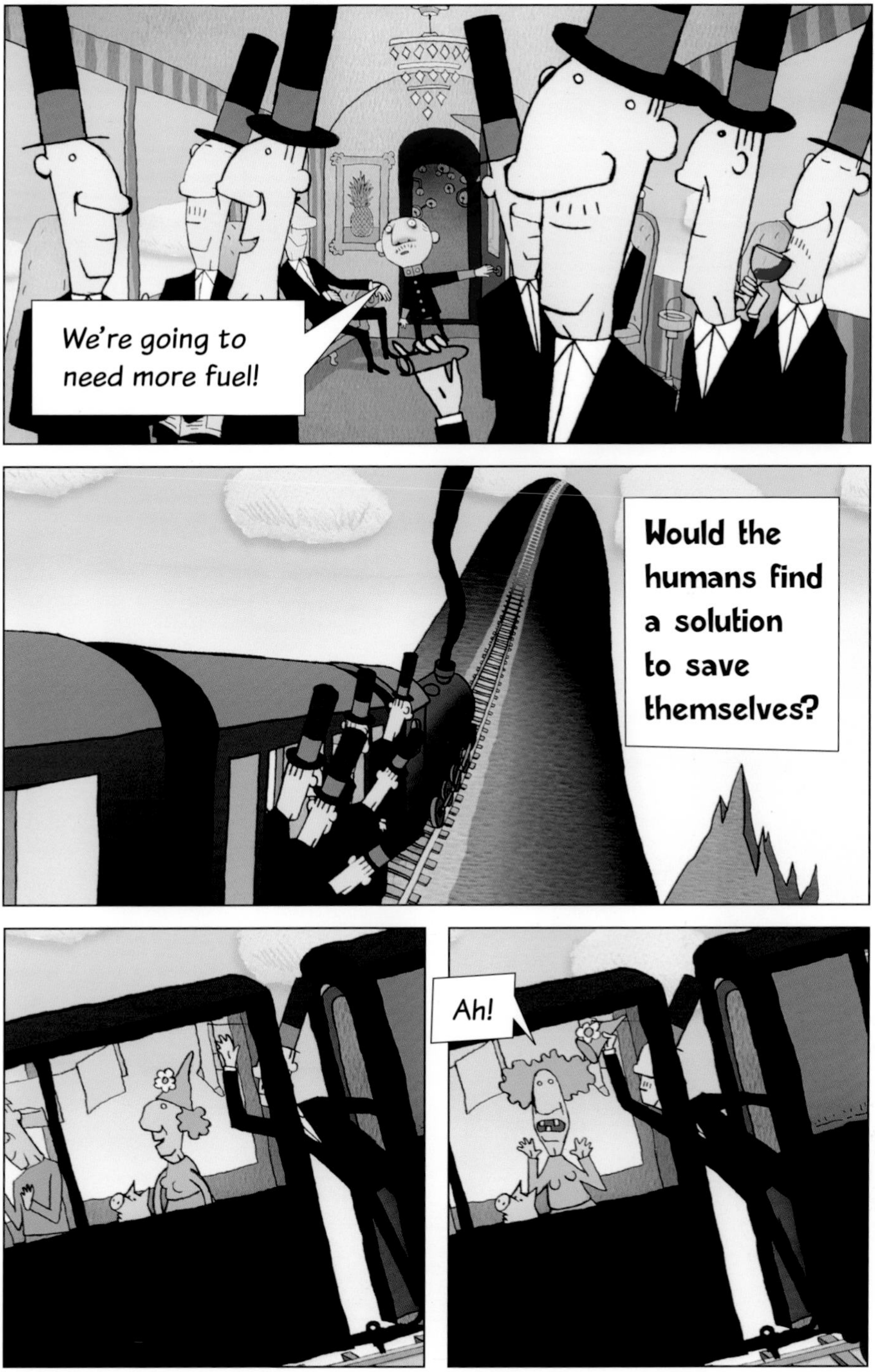
We're going to need more fuel!
Would the humans find a solution to save themselves?
Ah!

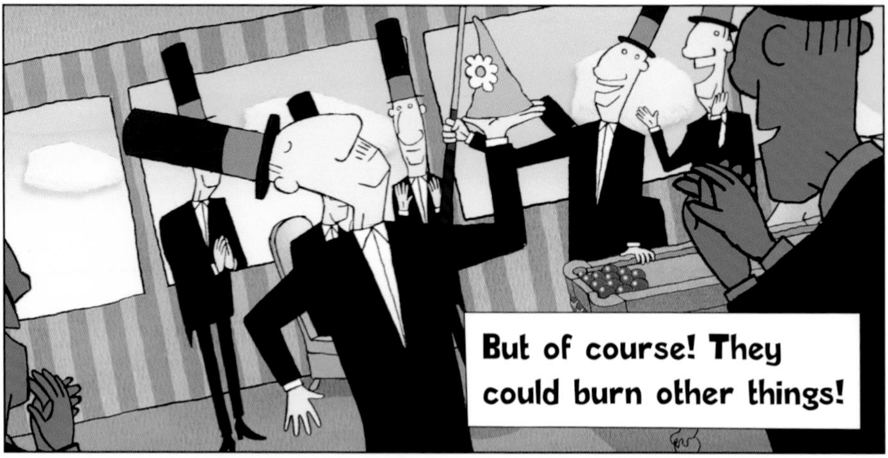
But of course! They could burn other things!

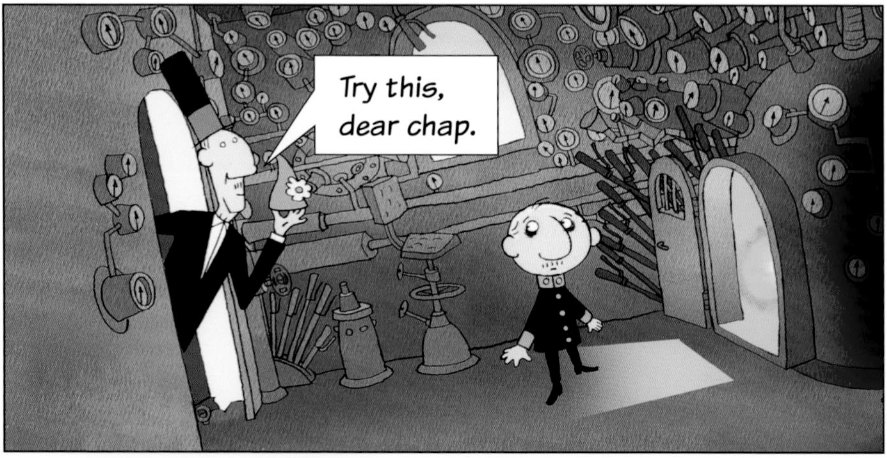
Try this, dear chap.

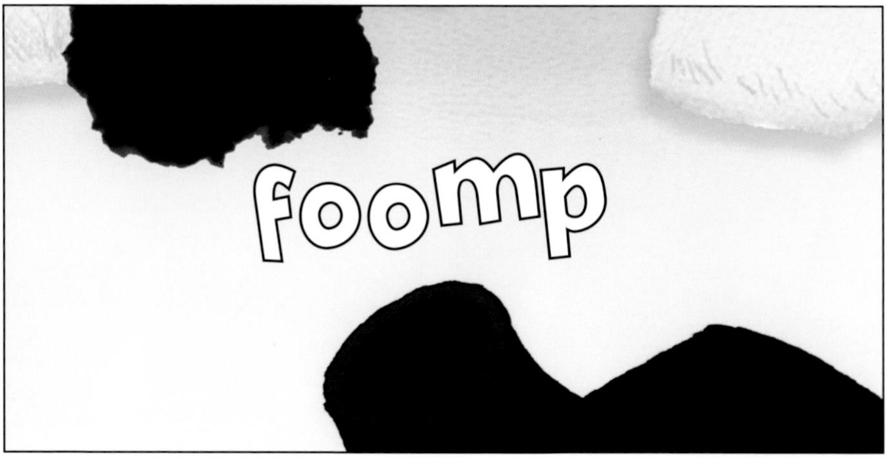
foomp

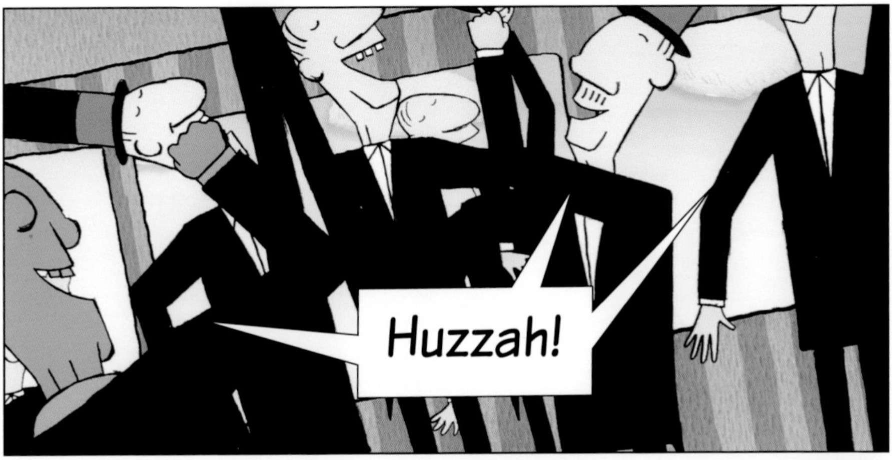
Huzzah!

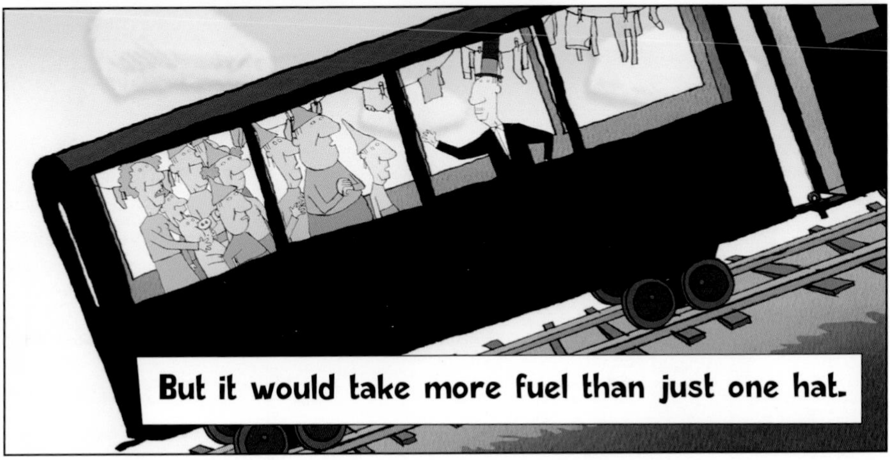
But it would take more fuel than just one hat.

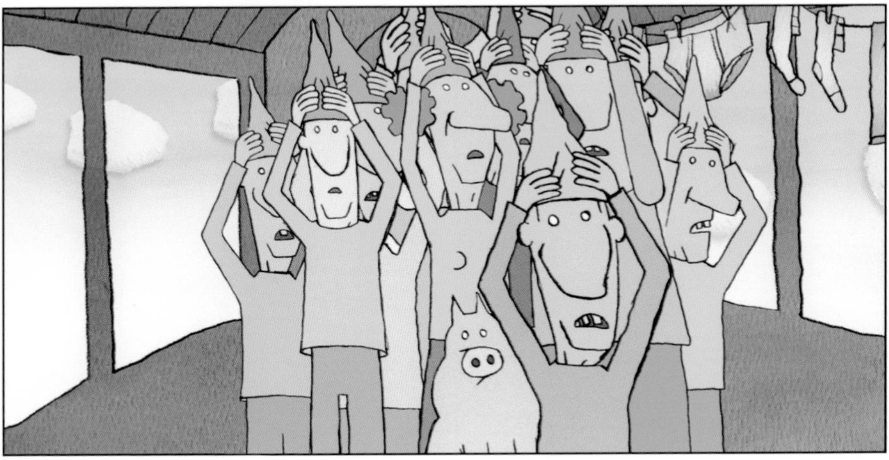

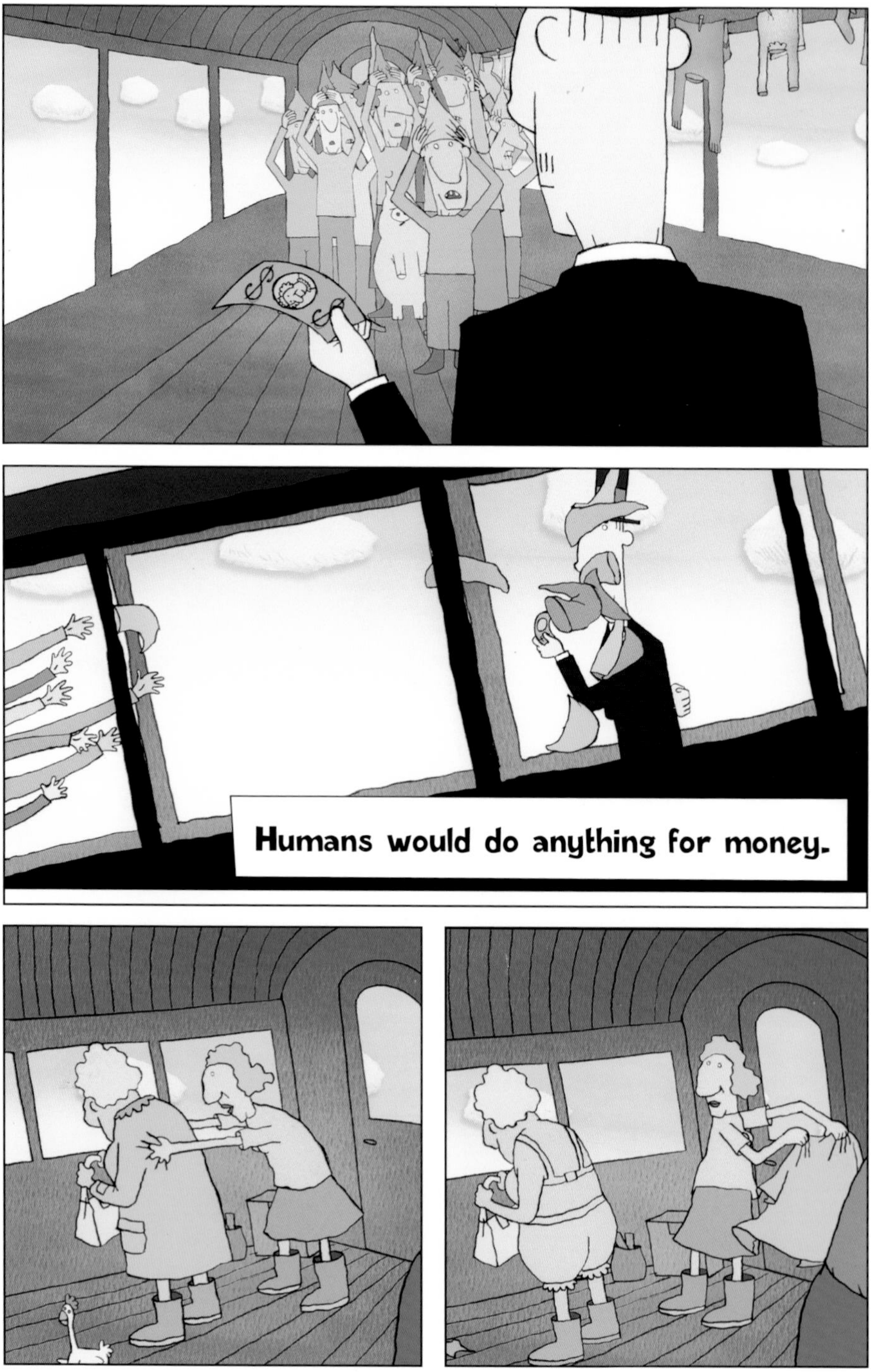
Humans would do anything for money.

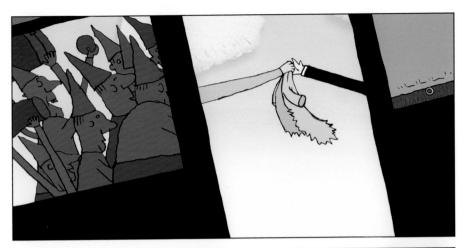

There goes the assembly line.

They all worked together to save themselves.

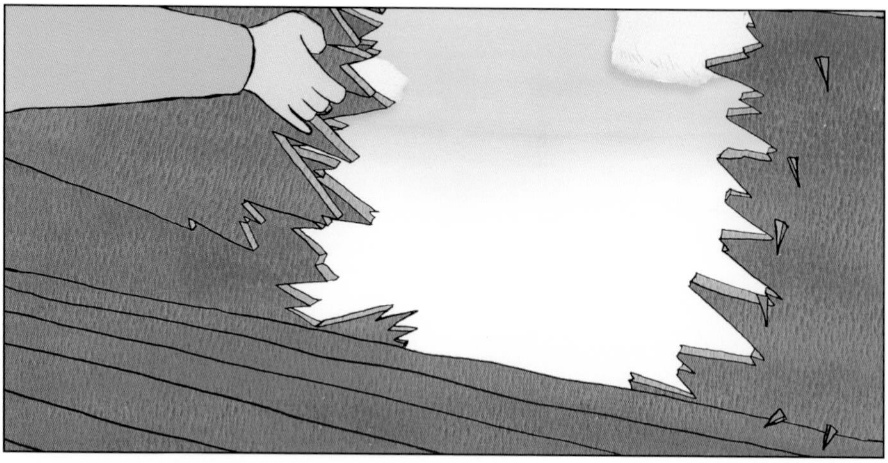

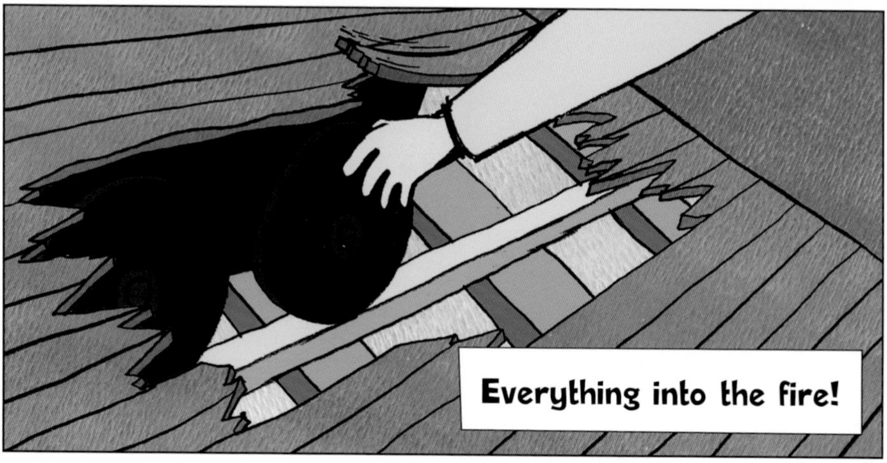
Everything into the fire!

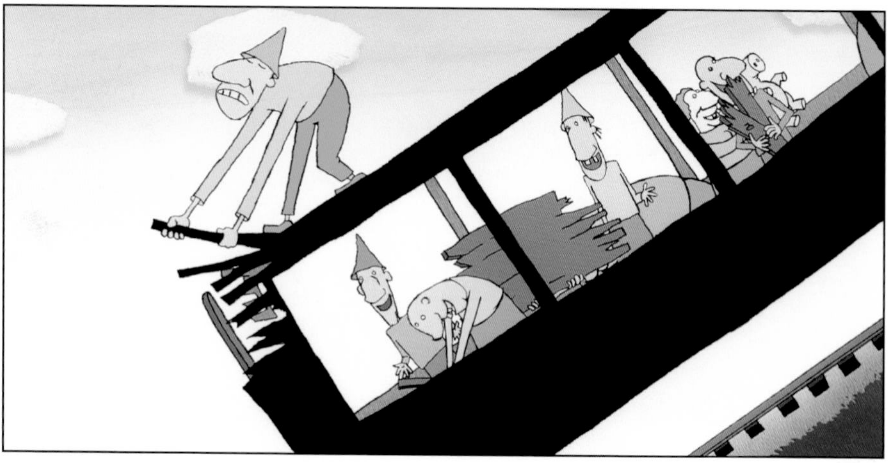

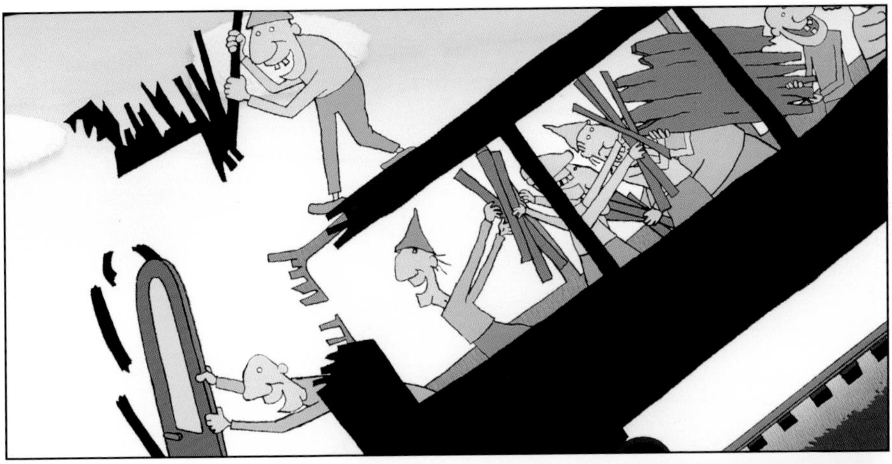

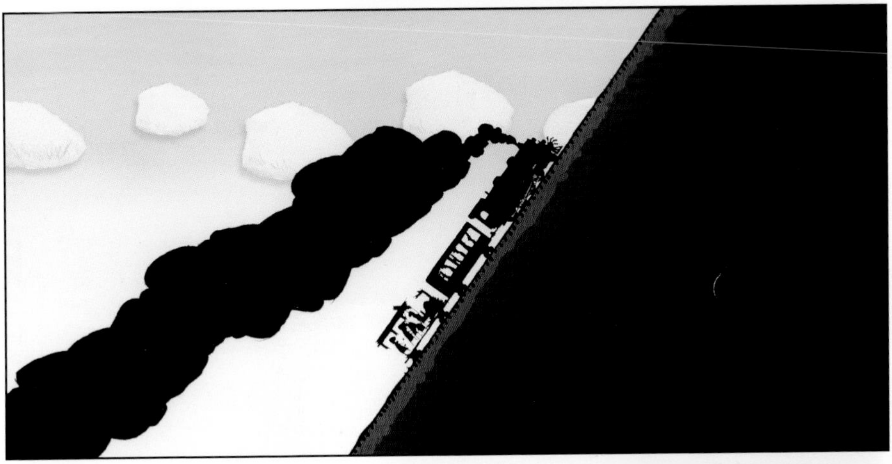

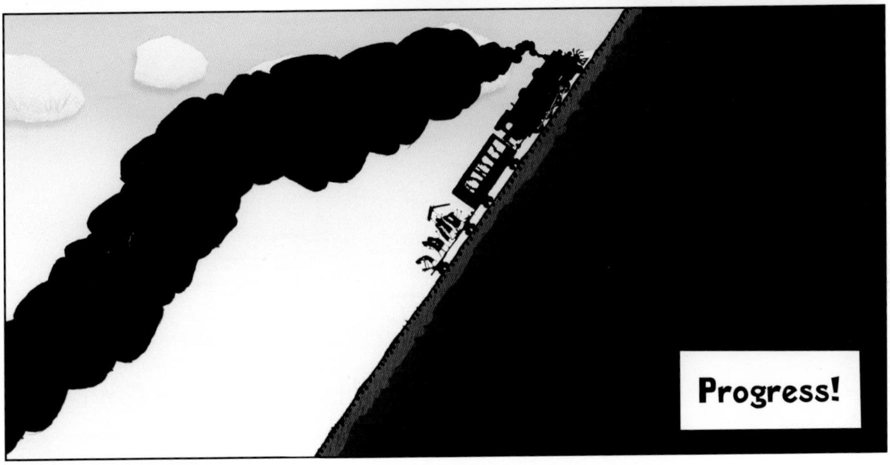
Progress!

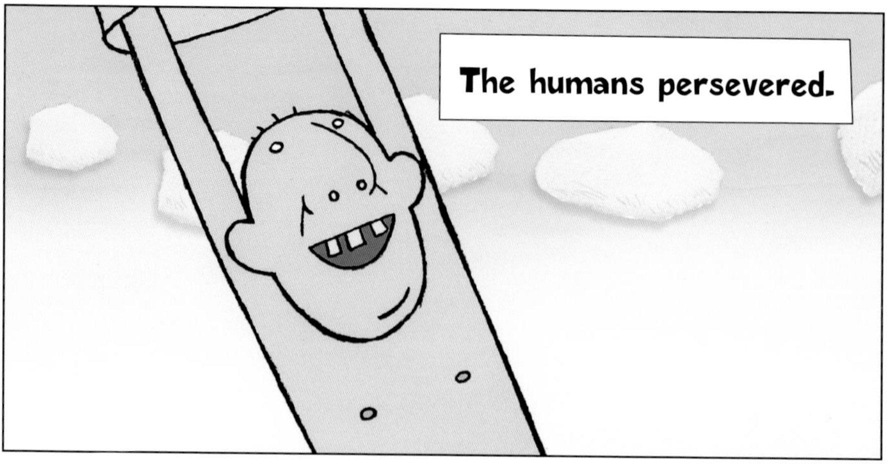
The humans persevered.

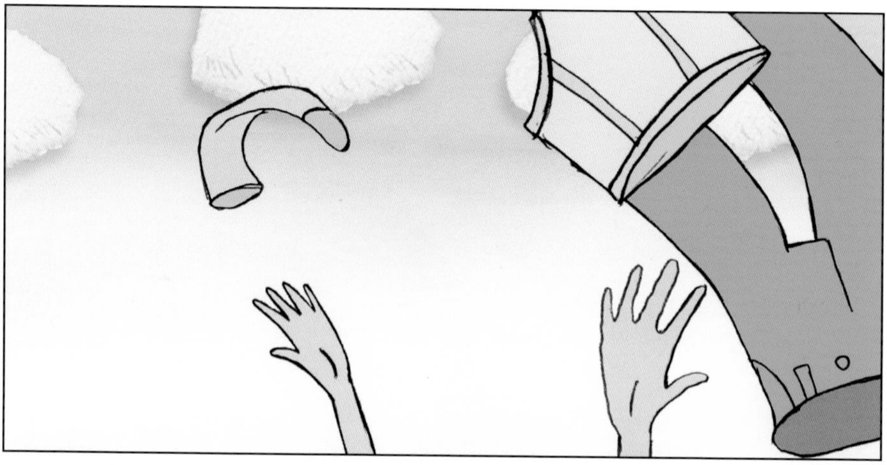

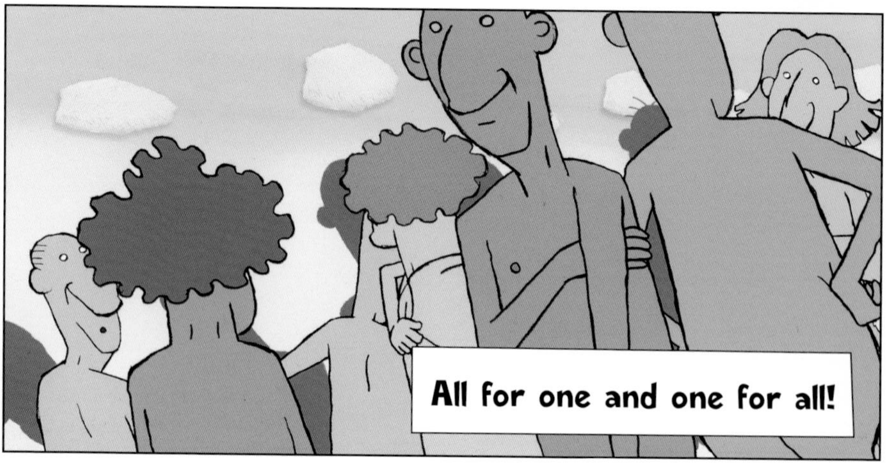
All for one and one for all!

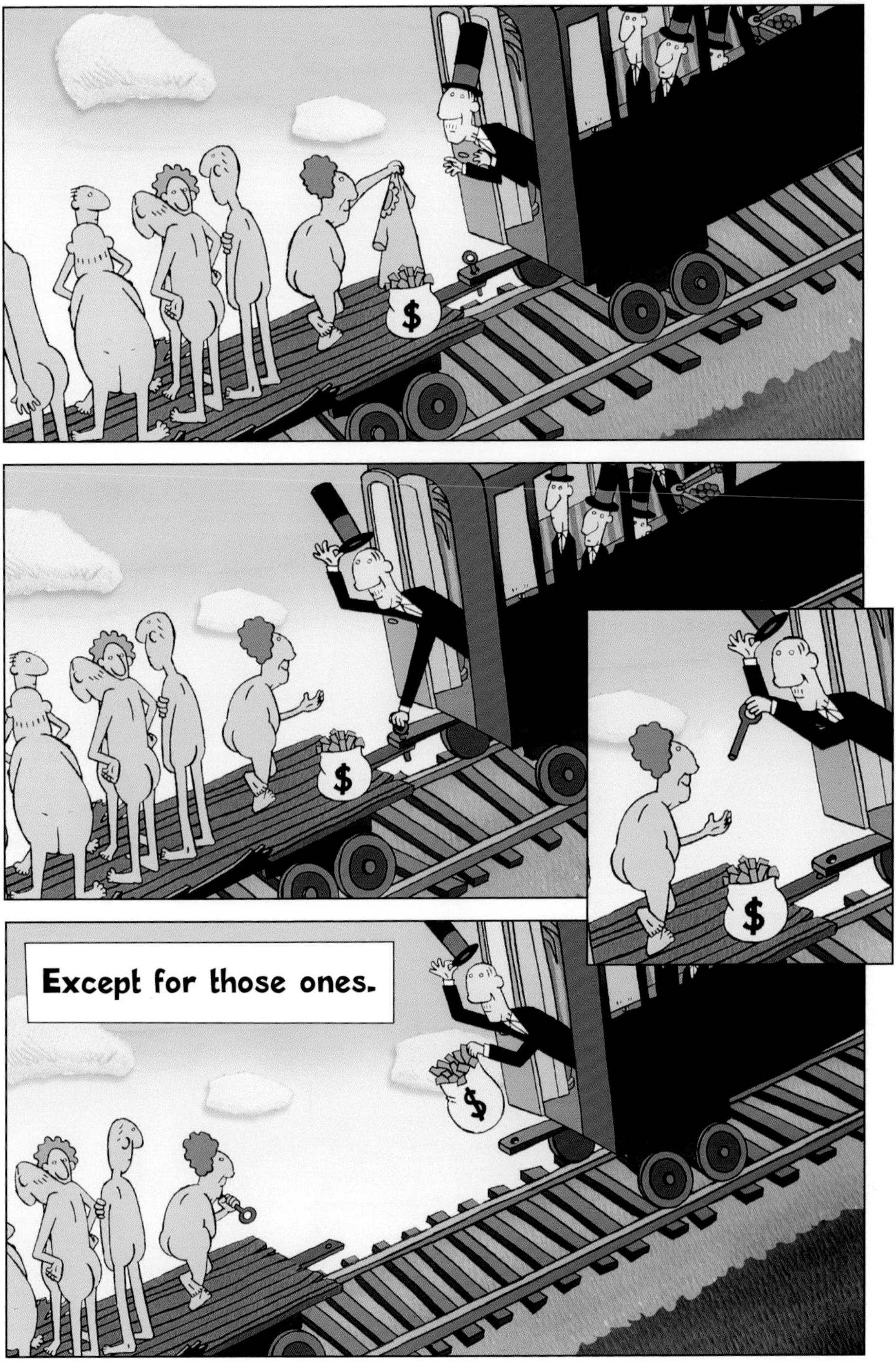
Except for those ones.

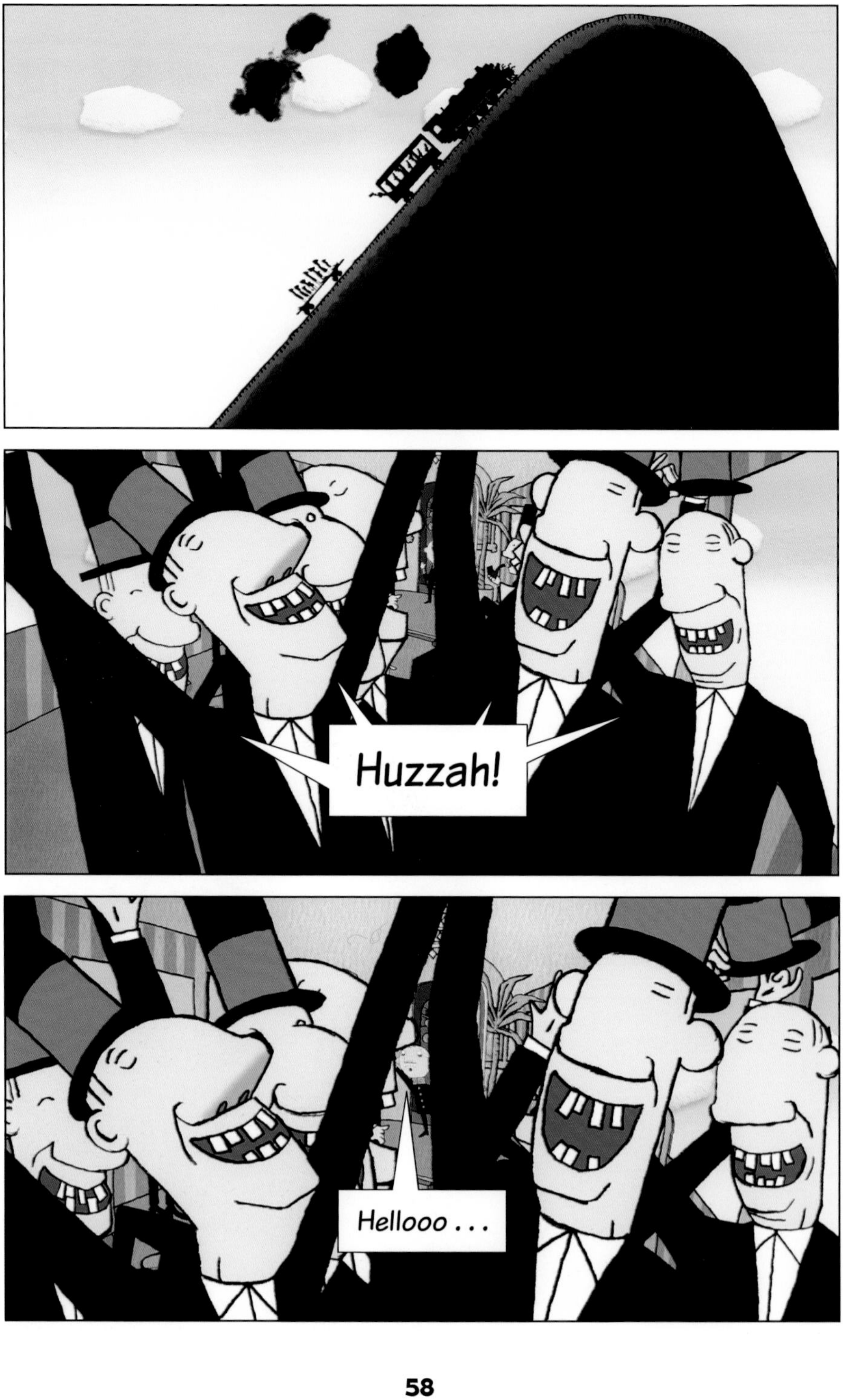
Huzzah!
Hellooo . . .

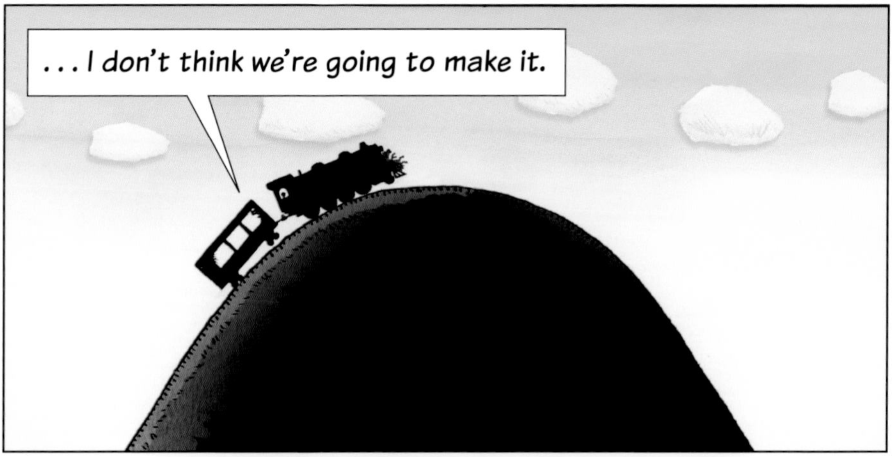
. . . I don't think we're going to make it.

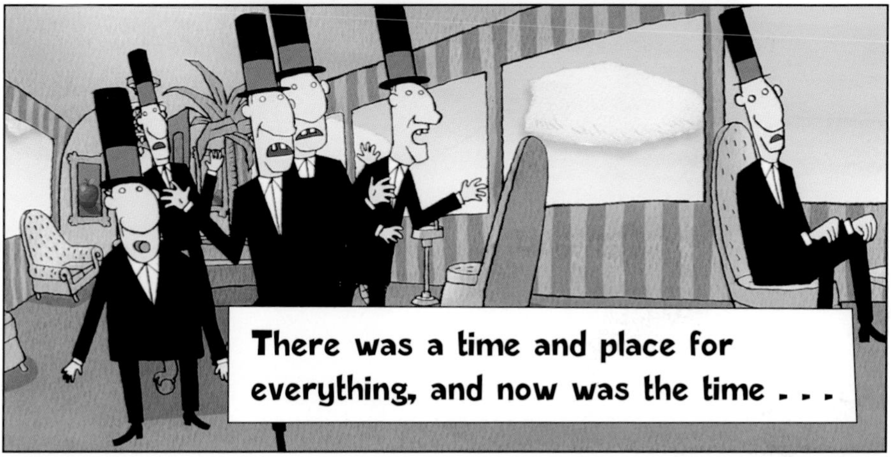
There was a time and place for everything, and now was the time . . .

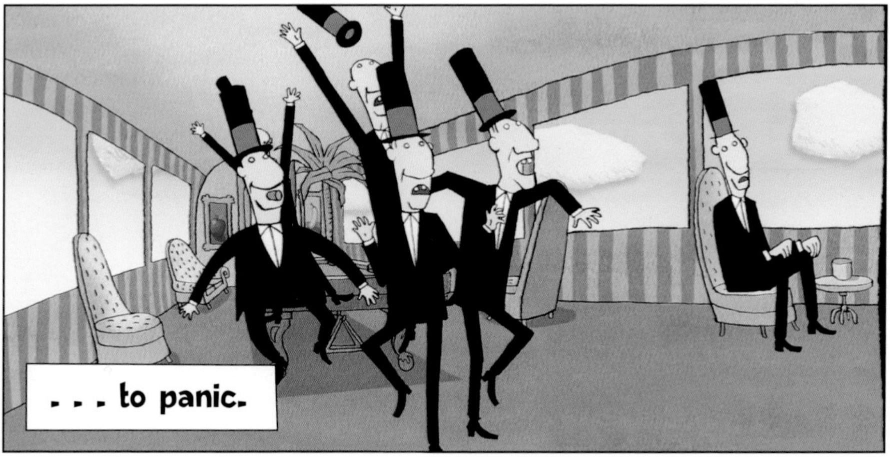
. . . to panic.

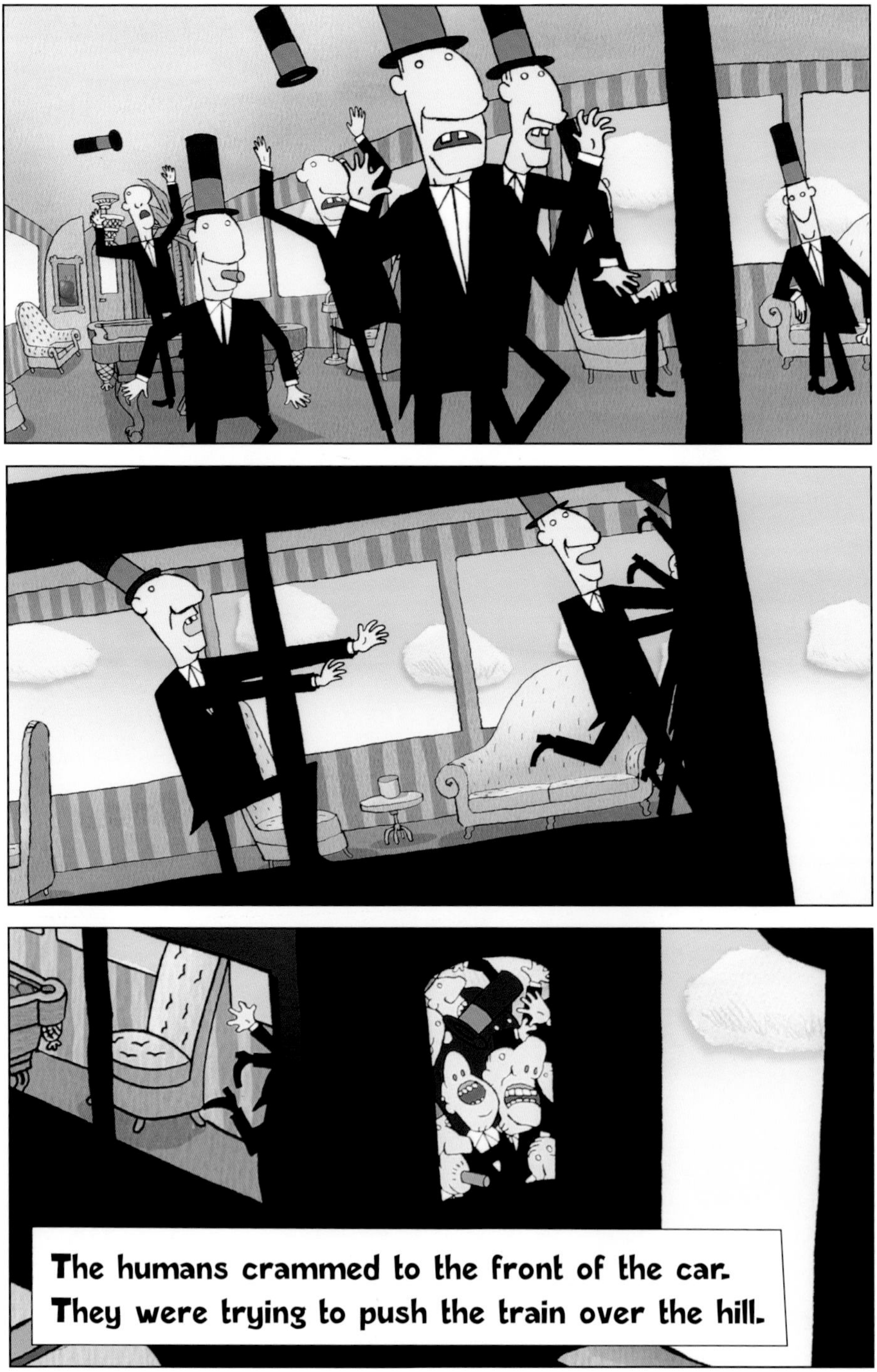
The humans crammed to the front of the car.
They were trying to push the train over the hill.

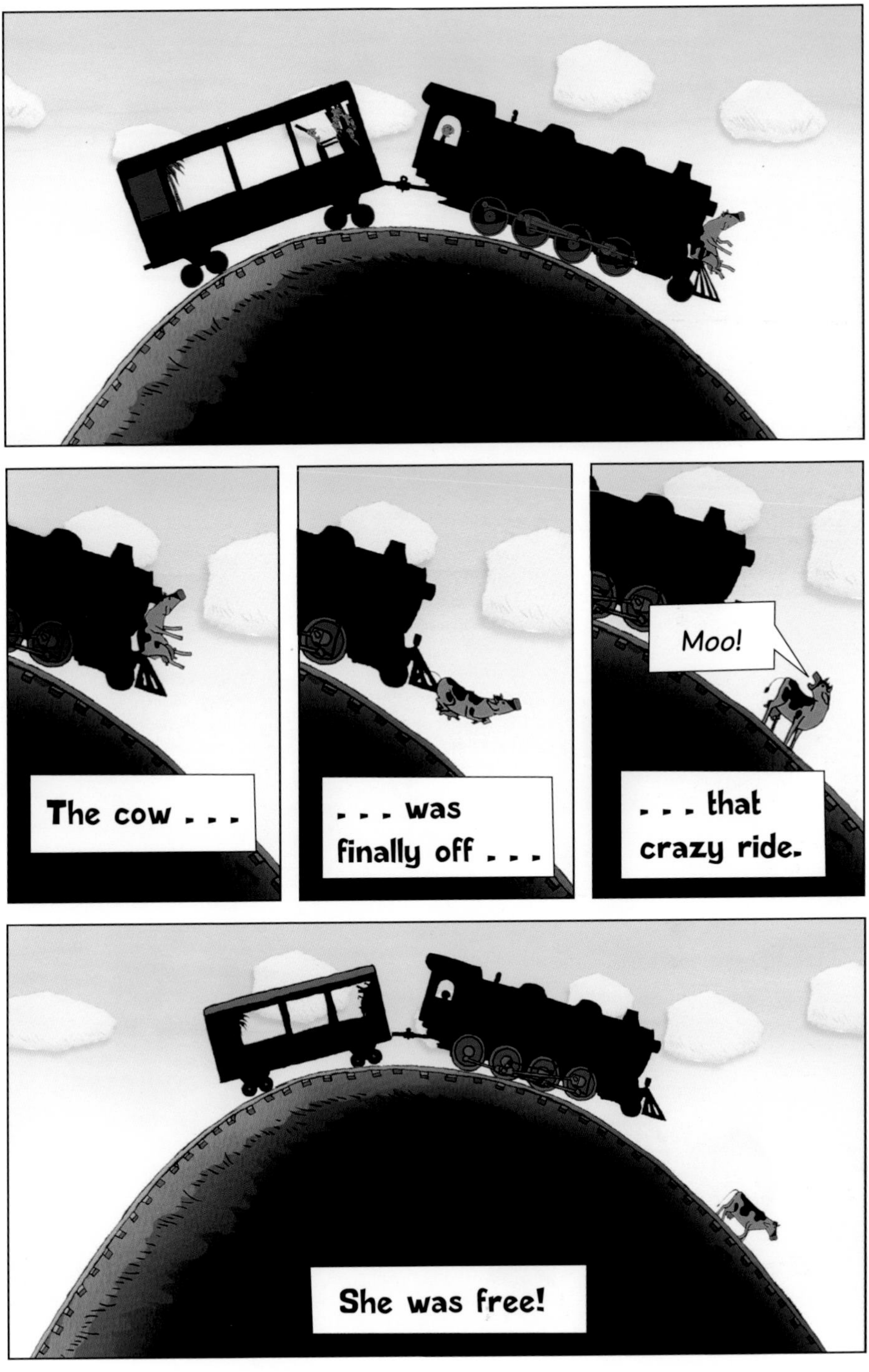
The cow . . .
. . . was finally off . . .
Moo!
. . . that crazy ride.
She was free!

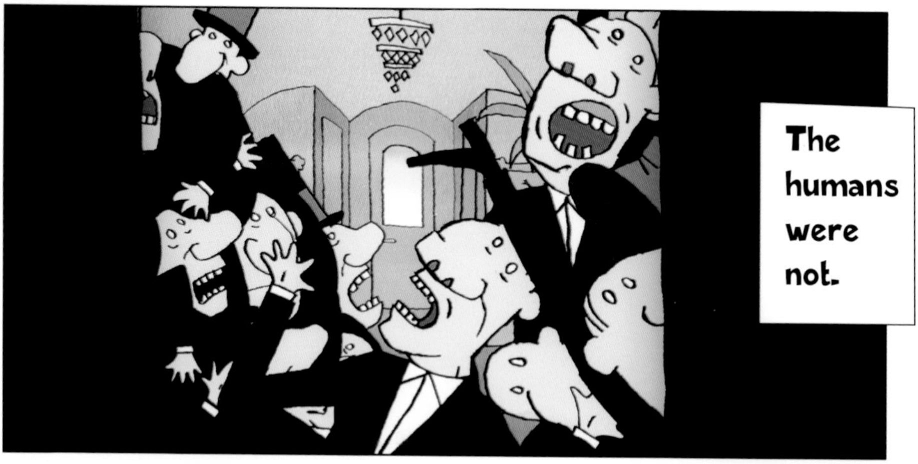
The humans were not.

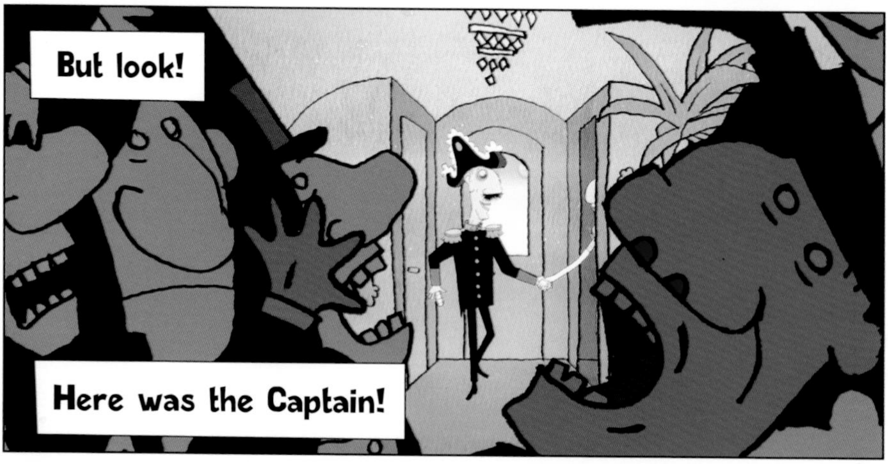
But look!
Here was the Captain!

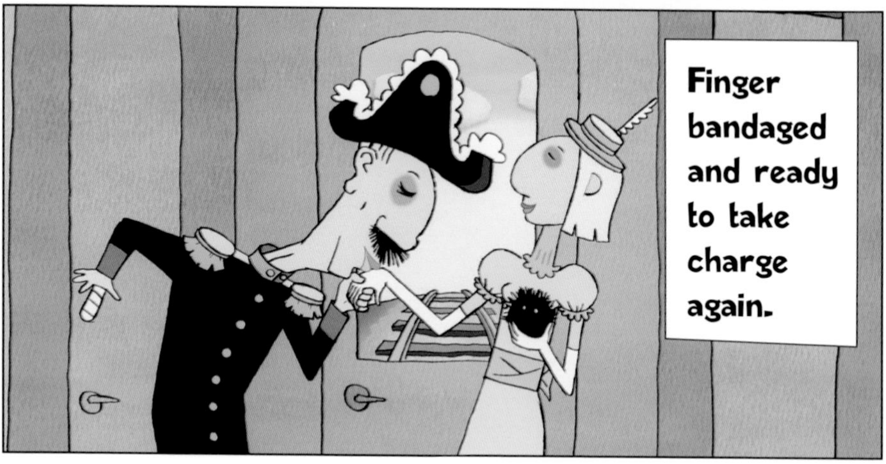
Finger bandaged and ready to take charge again.

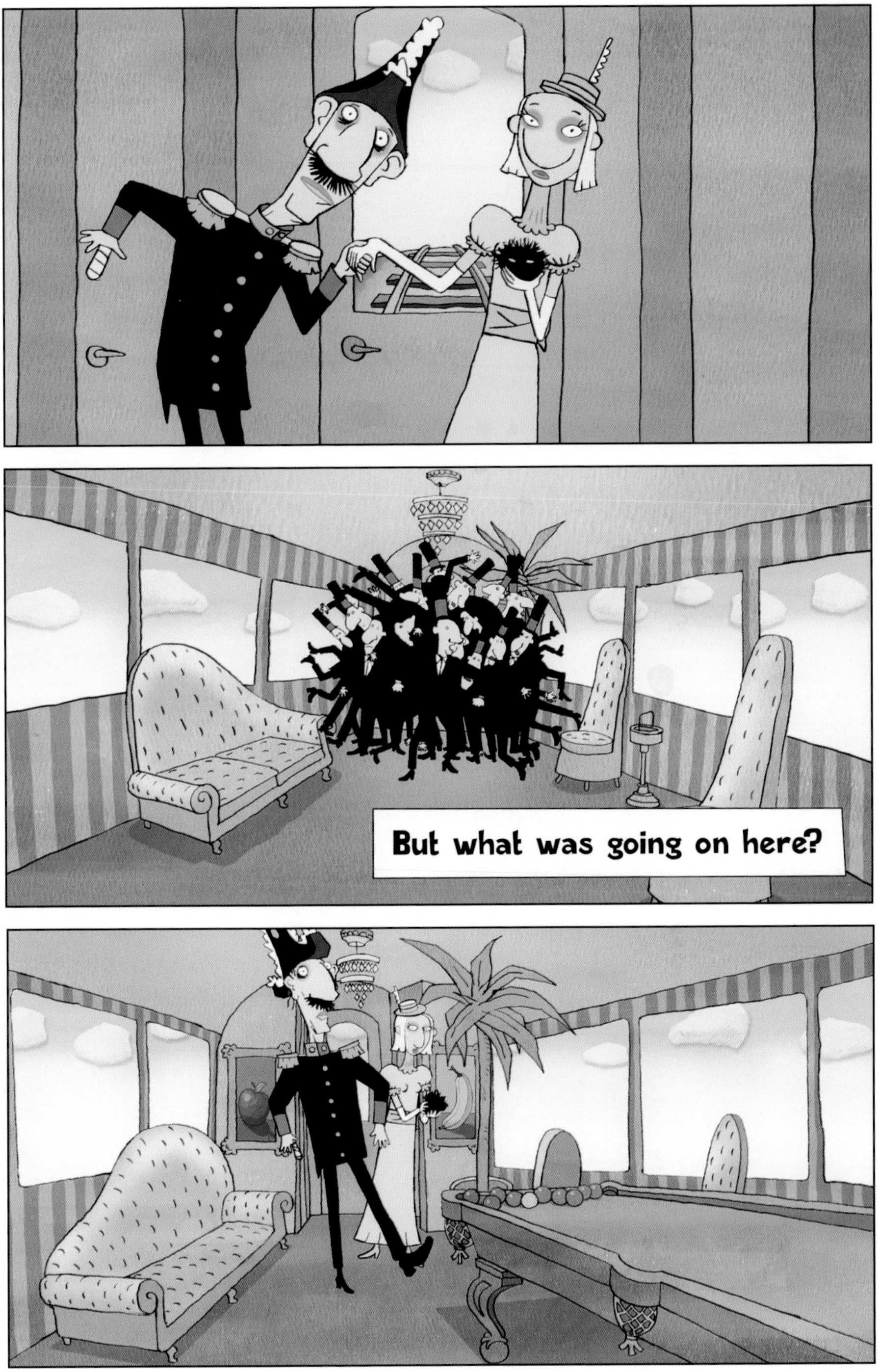
But what was going on here?

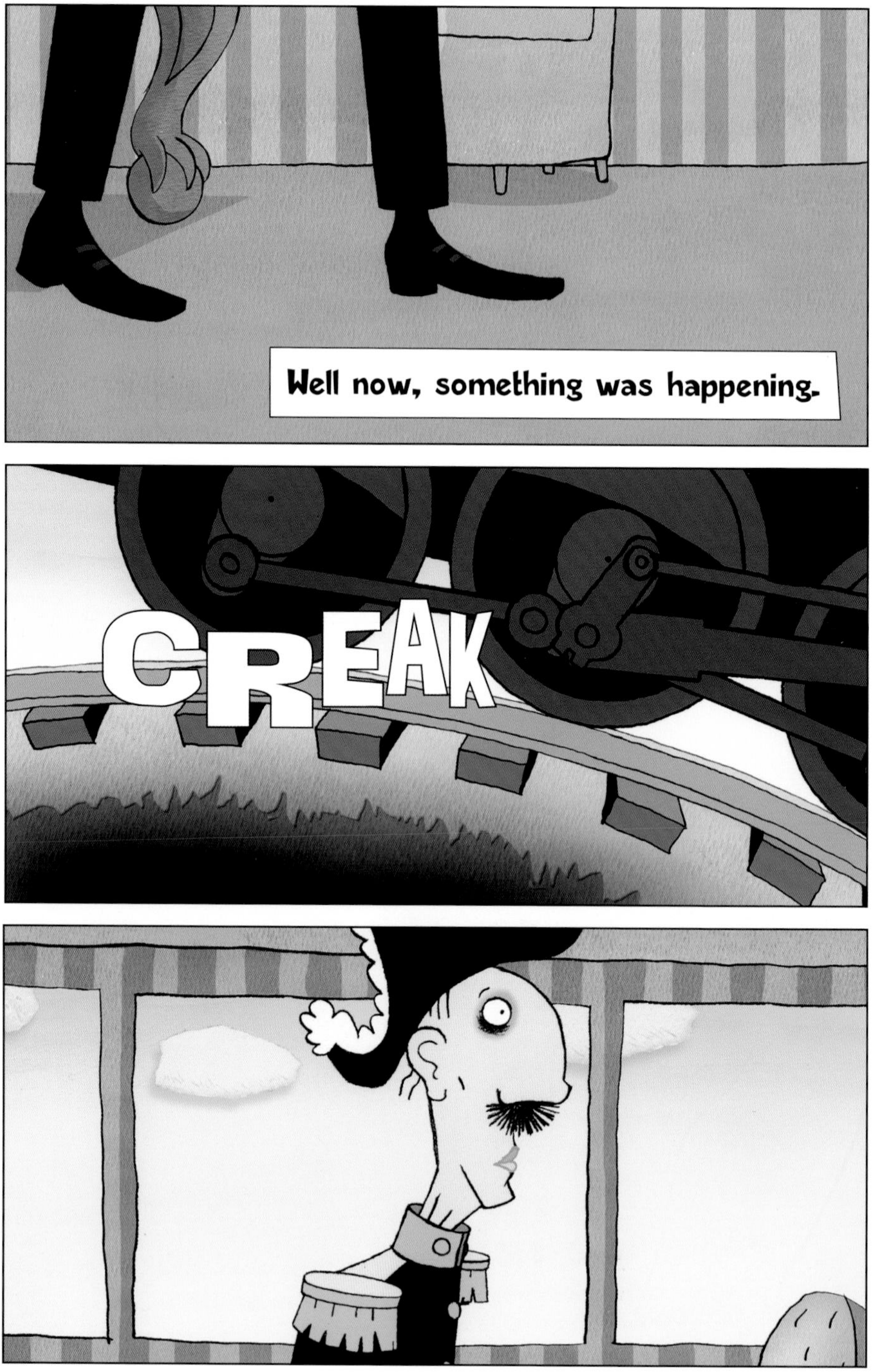
Well now, something was happening.
CREAK

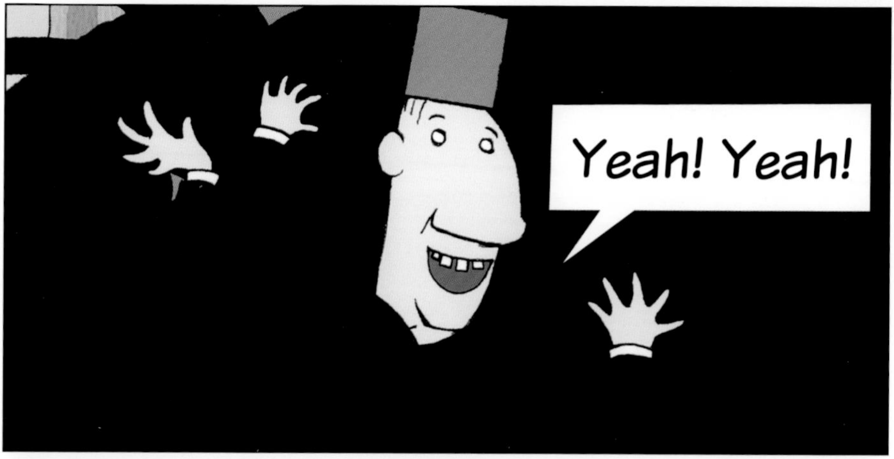
Yeah! Yeah!

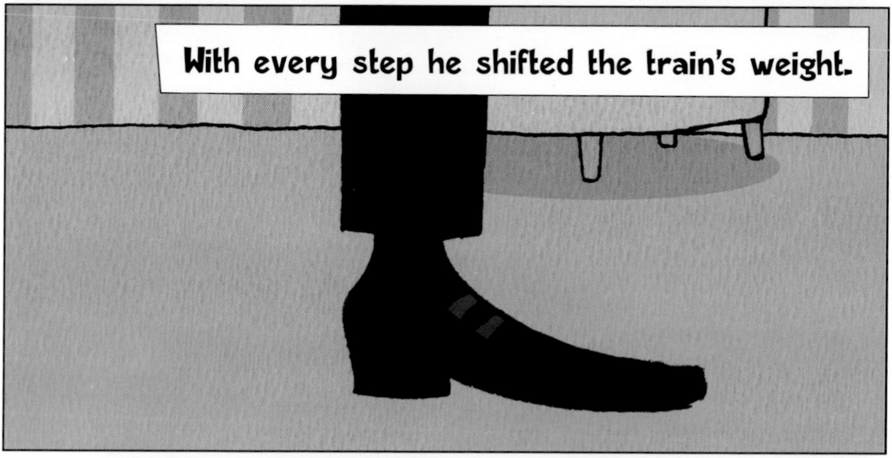
With every step he shifted the train's weight.

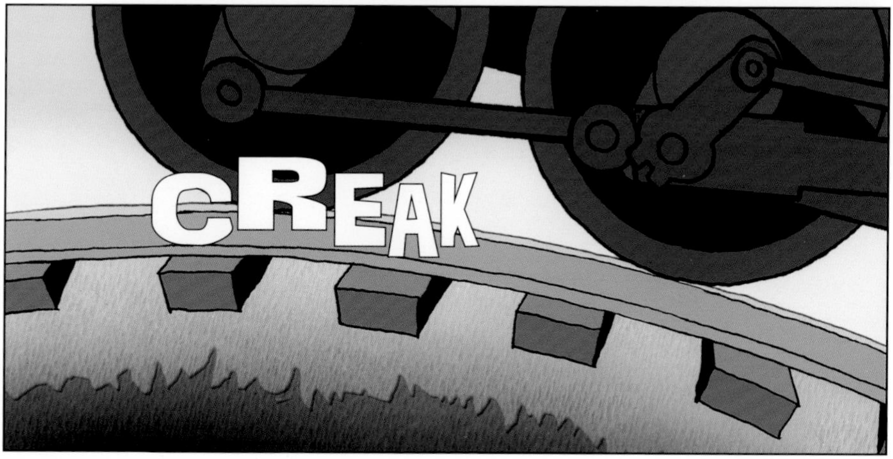
CREAK

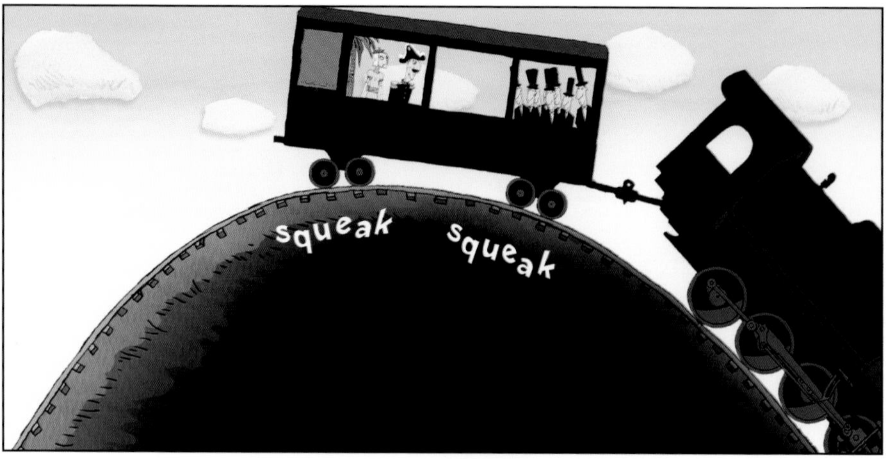
squeak
squeak

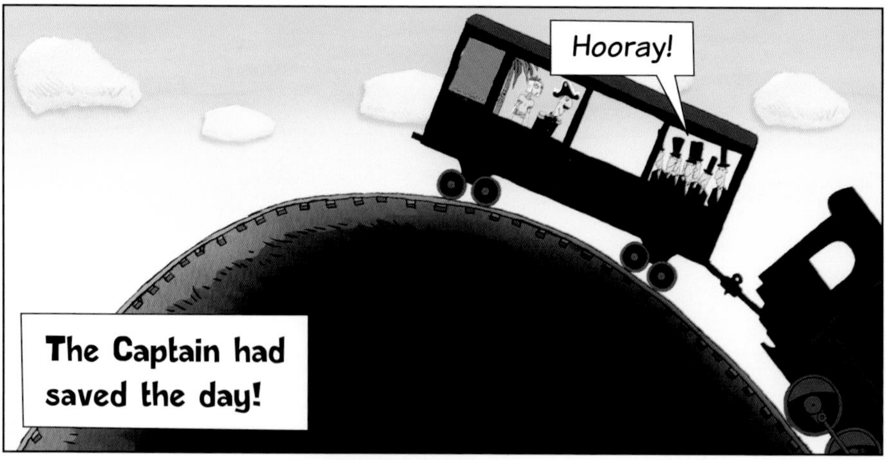
Hooray!
The Captain had saved the day!

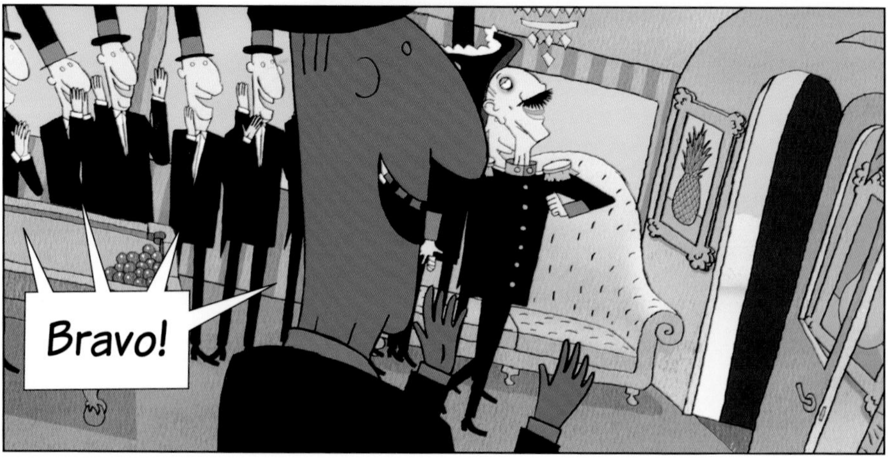
Bravo!

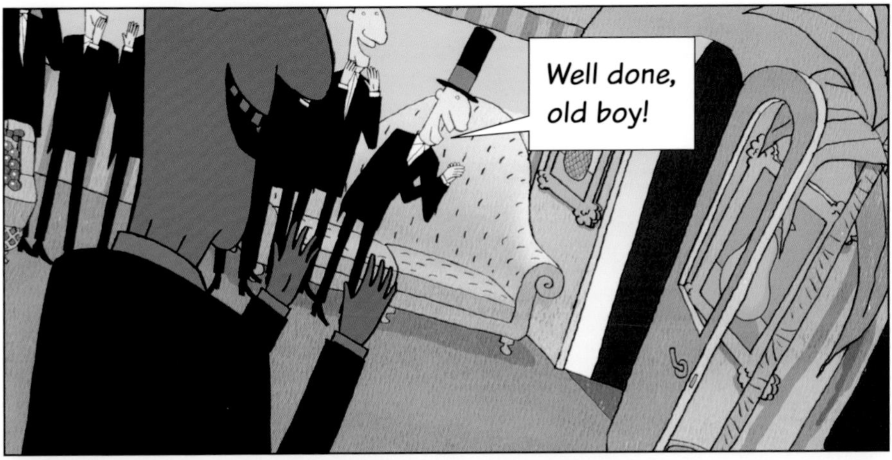
Well done,
old boy!

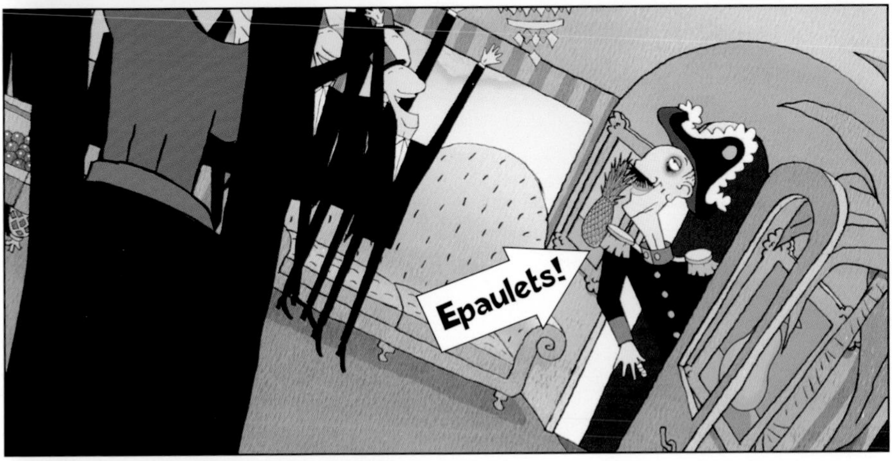
Epaulets!

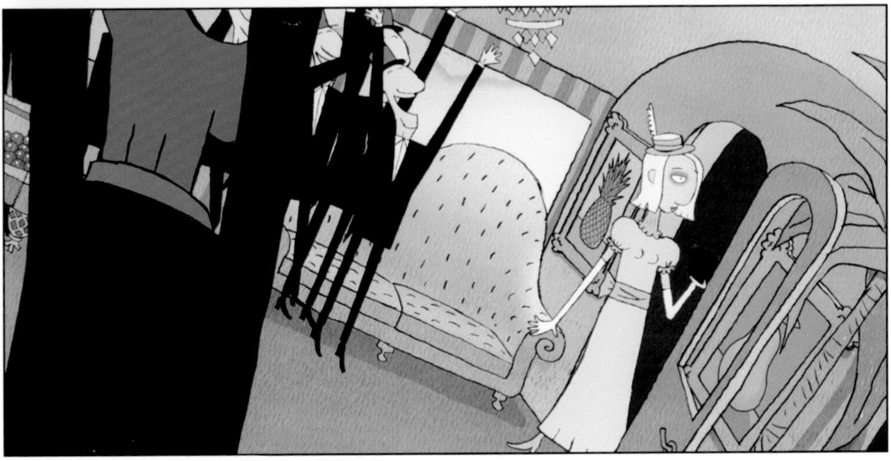

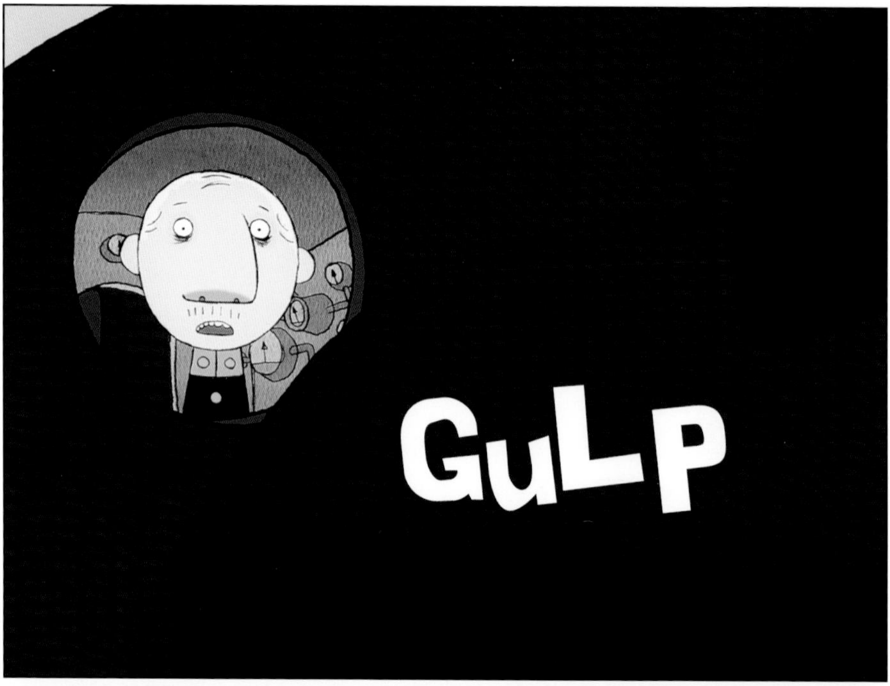
GuLP

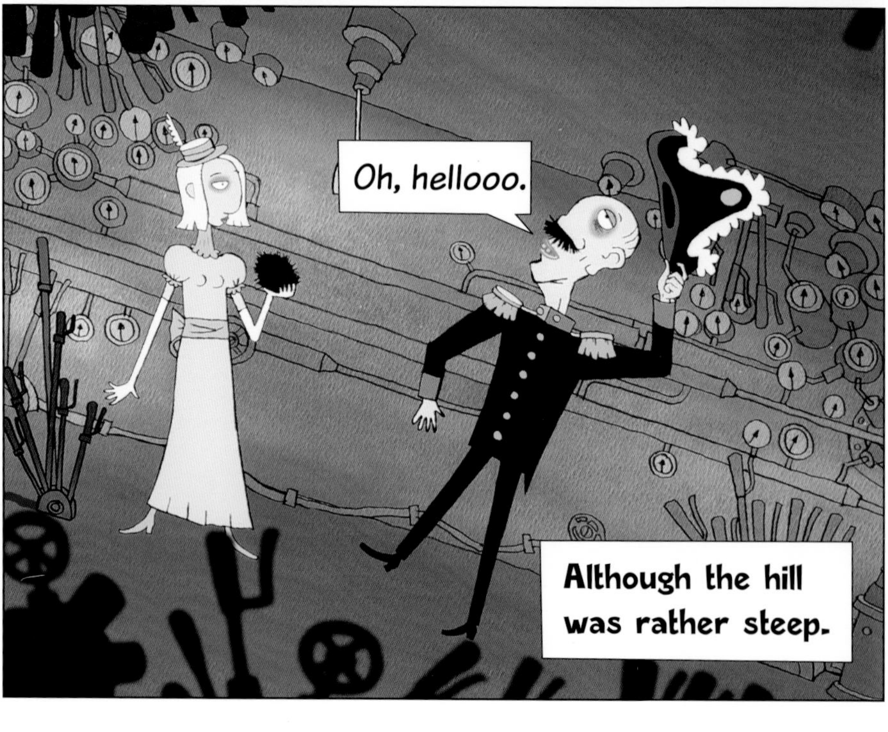
Oh, hellooo.
Although the hill was rather steep.

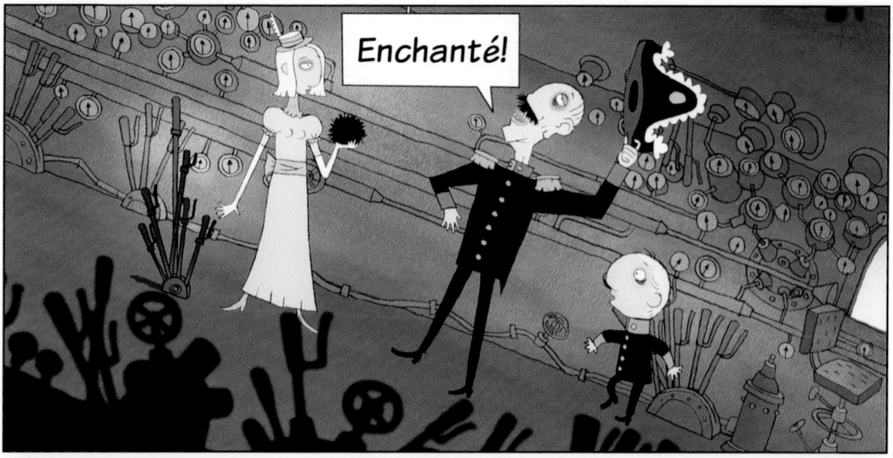
Enchanté!

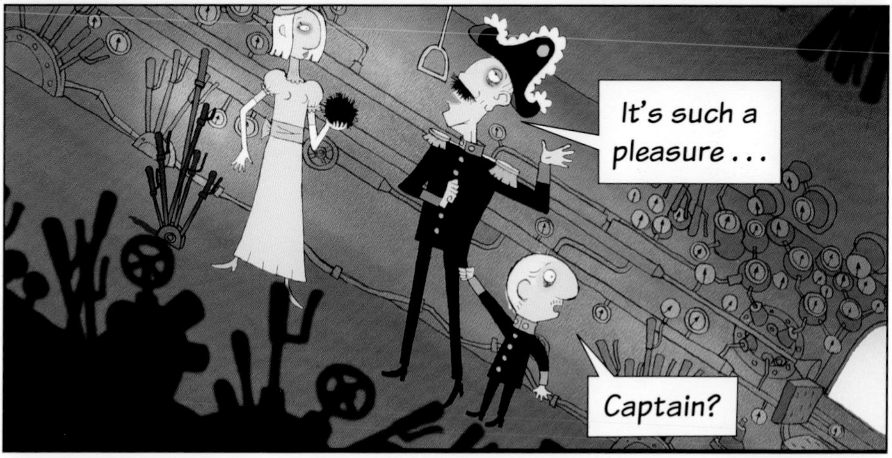
It's such a pleasure . . .
Captain?

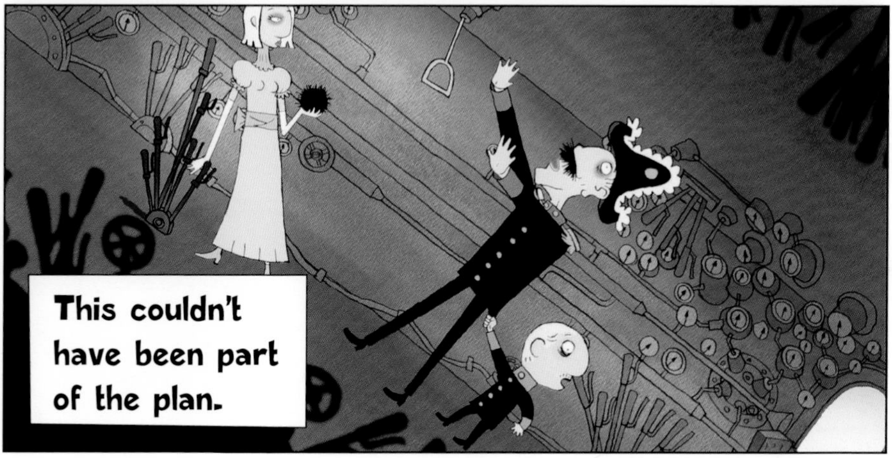
This couldn't have been part of the plan.

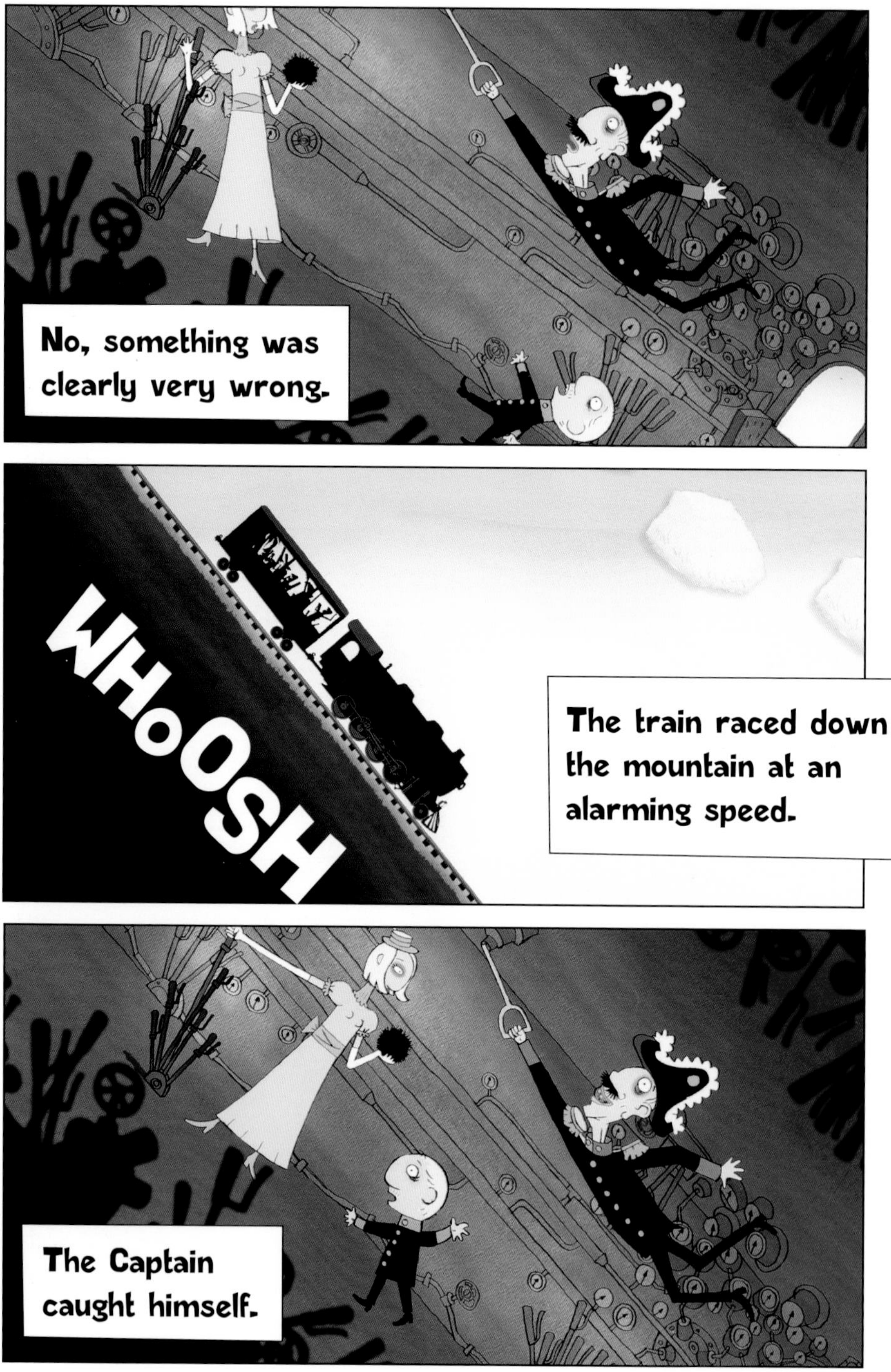
No, something was clearly very wrong.
WHoOSH
The train raced down the mountain at an alarming speed.
The Captain caught himself.

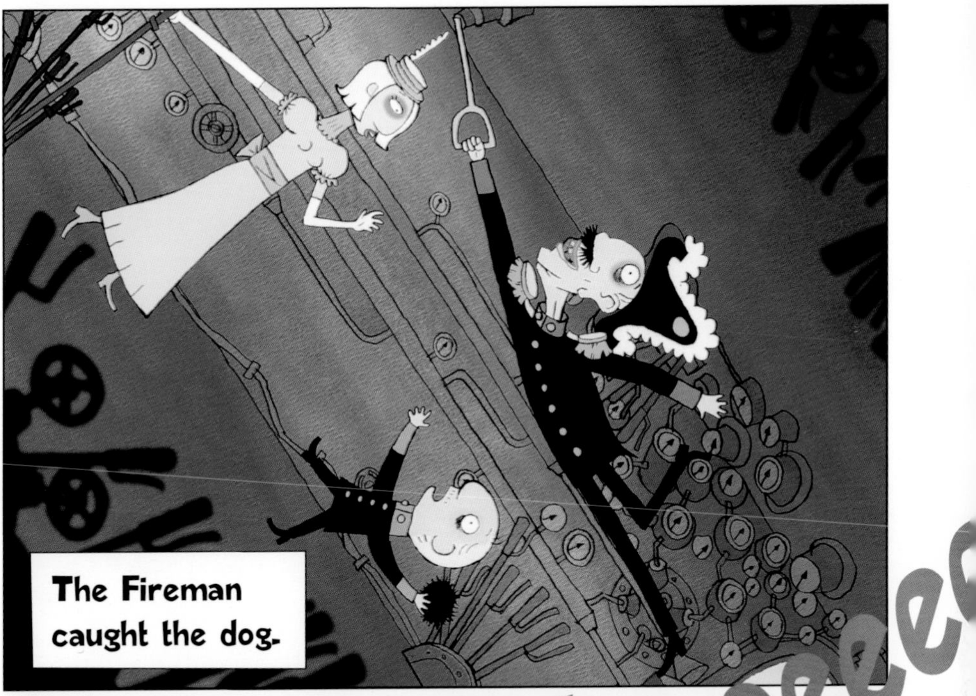
The Fireman caught the dog.

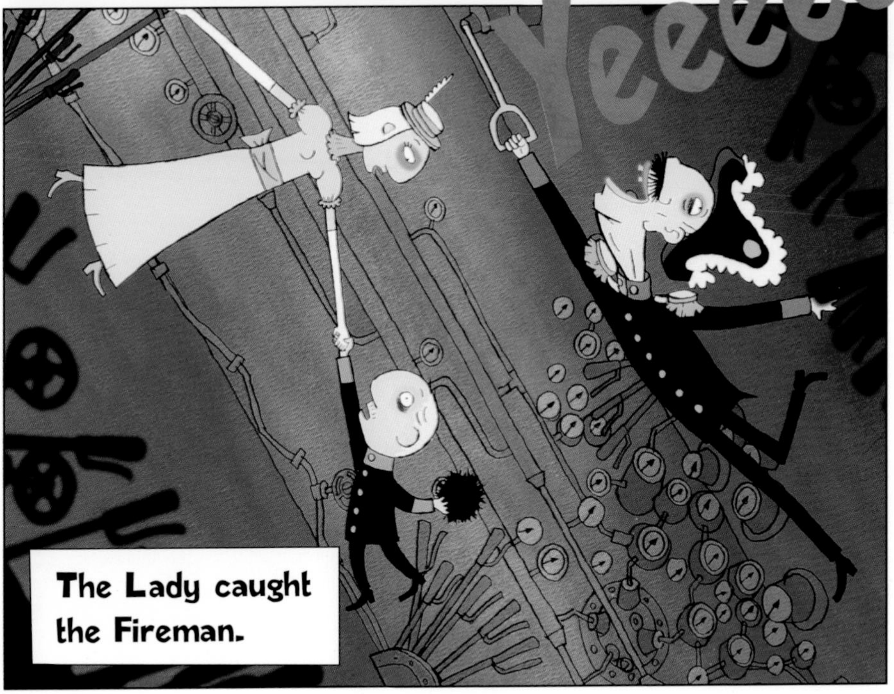
The Lady caught the Fireman.

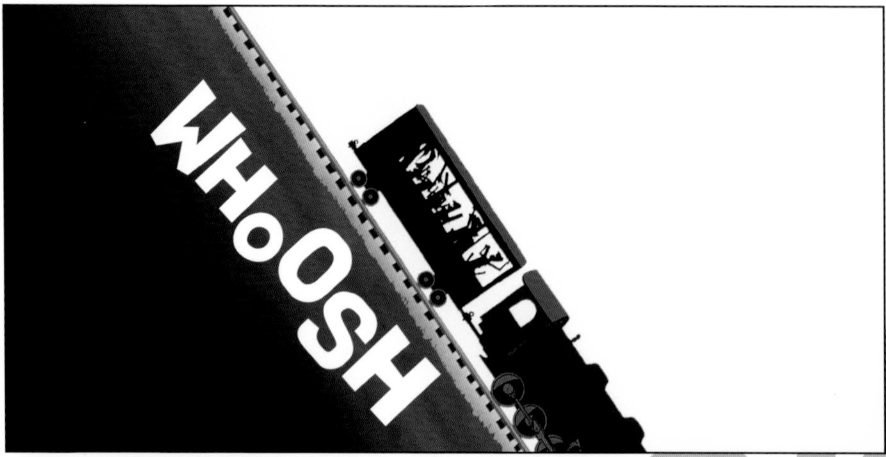
WHoOSH

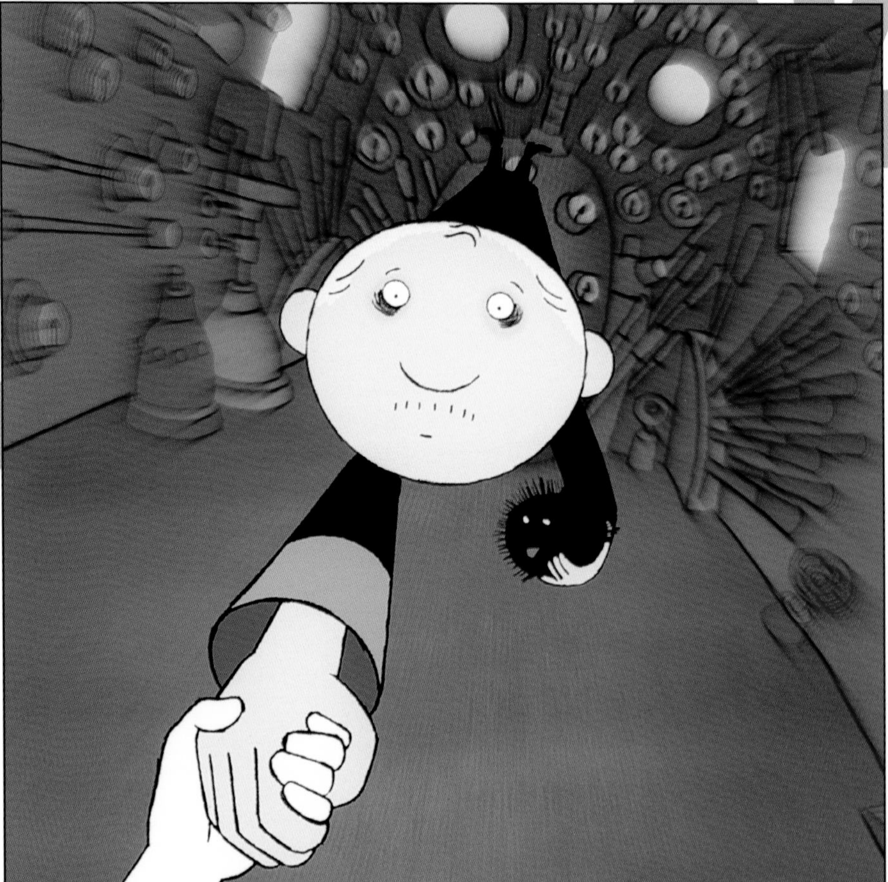

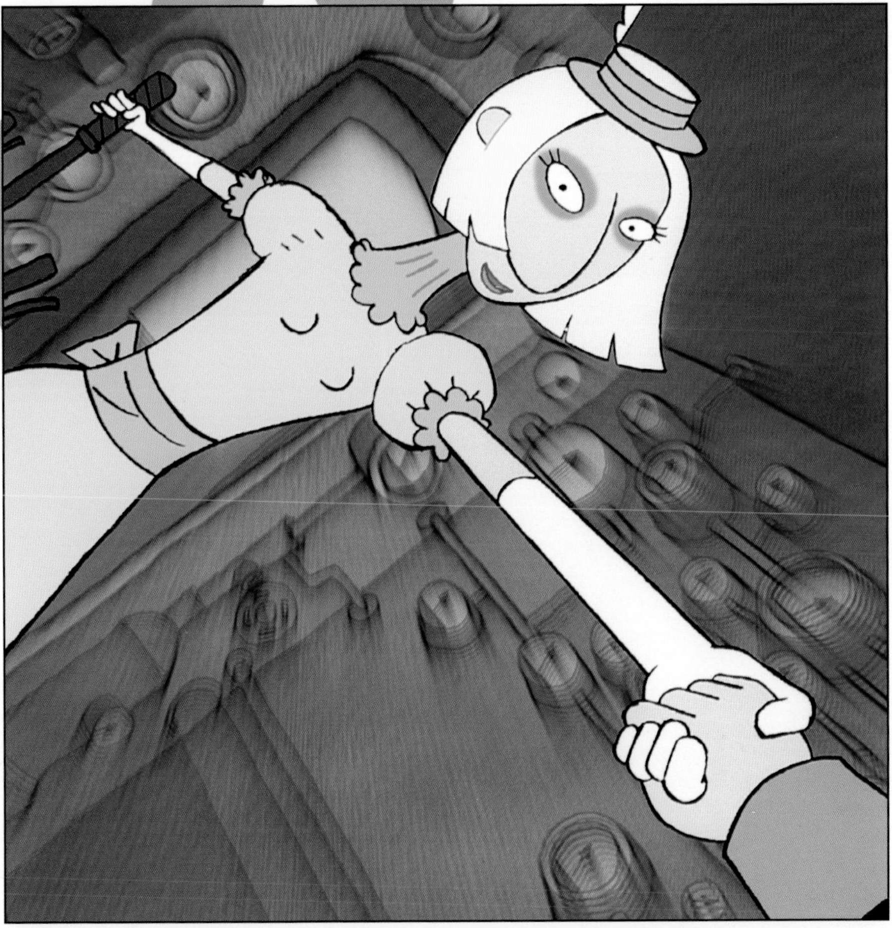

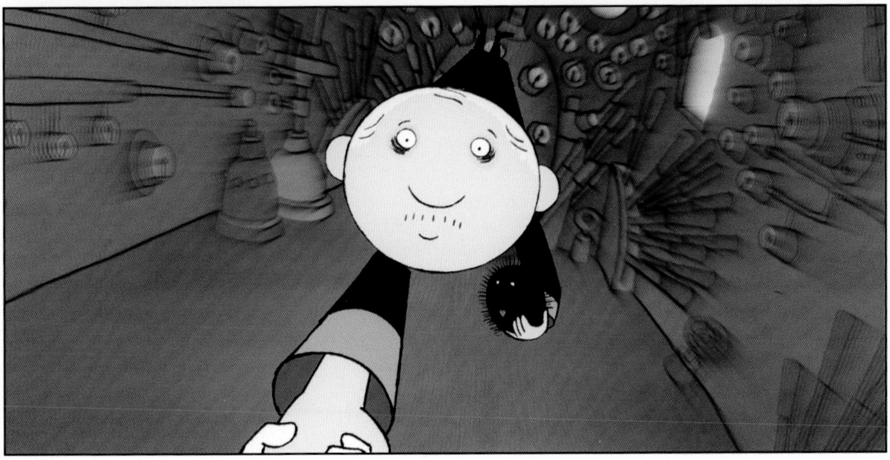

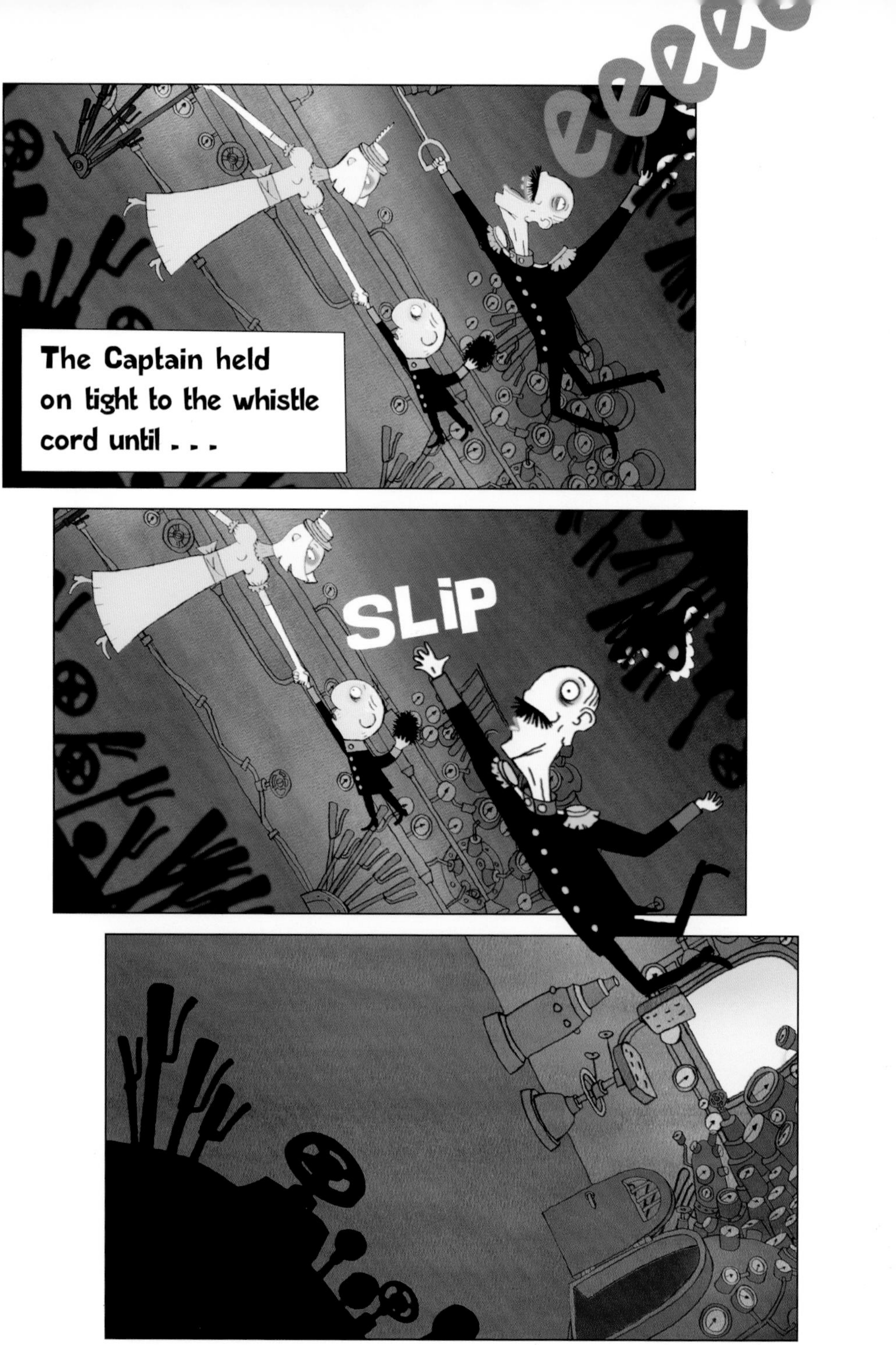
eeeee
The Captain held on tight to the whistle cord until . . .
SLIP

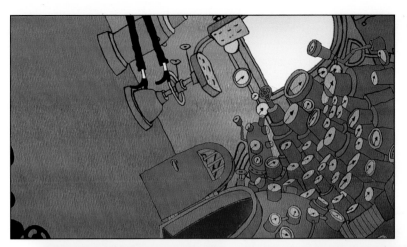

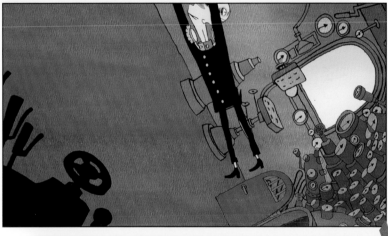

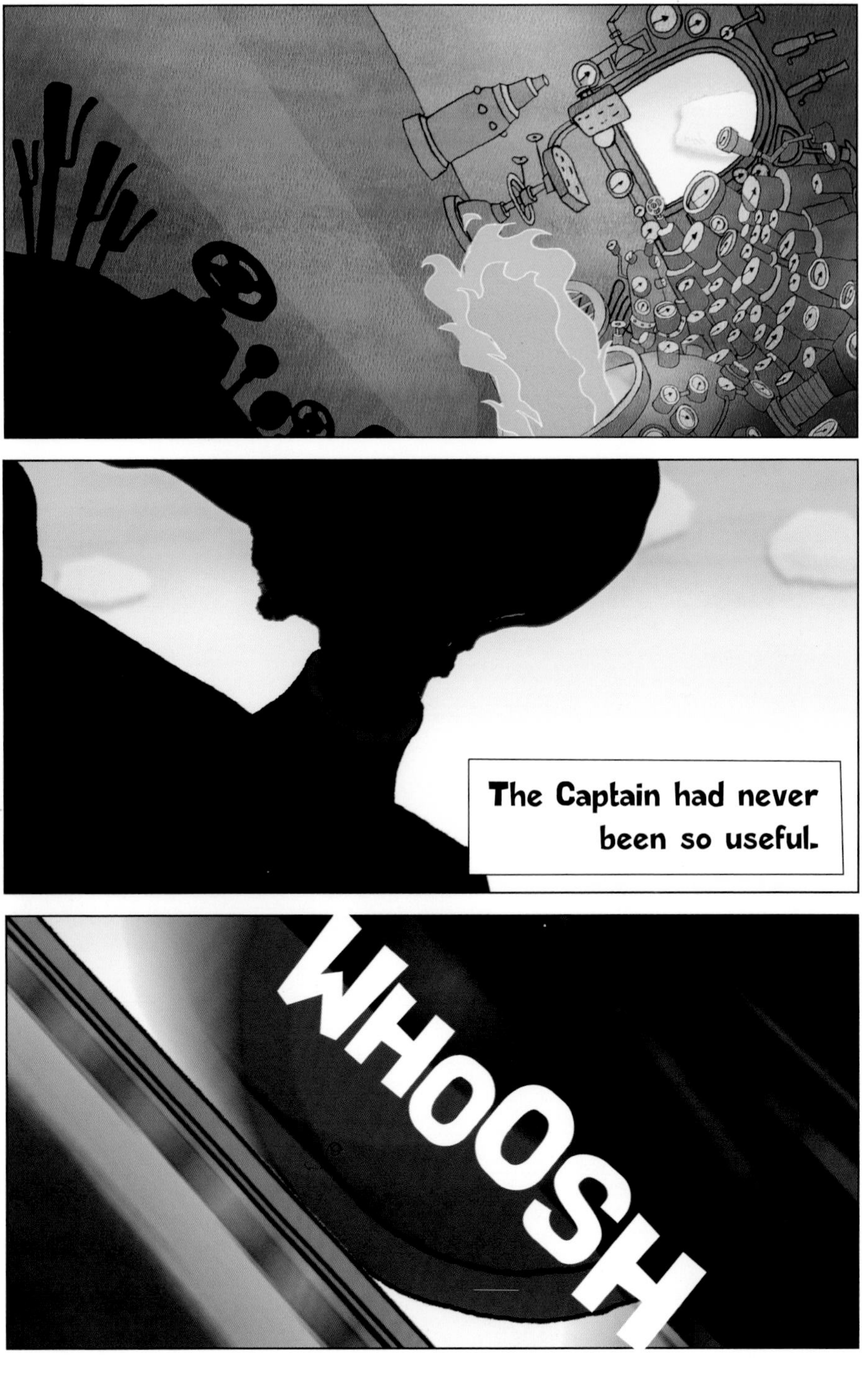
The Captain had never been so useful.
WHOOSH

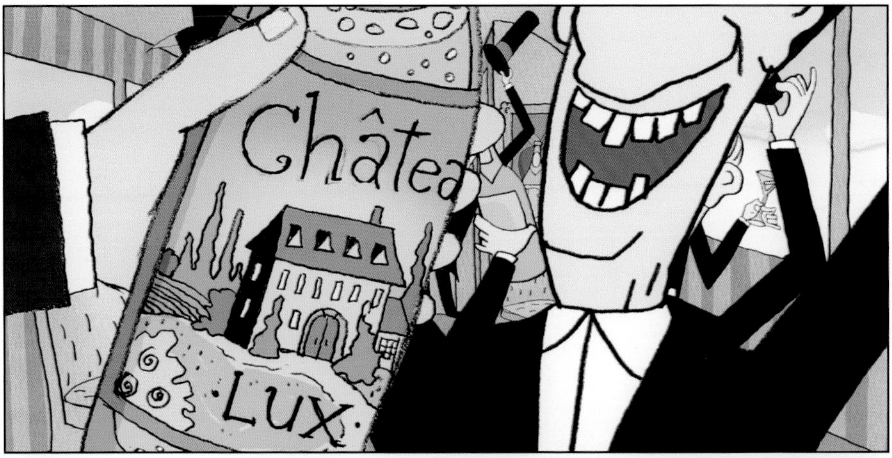
Châtea
·Lux·

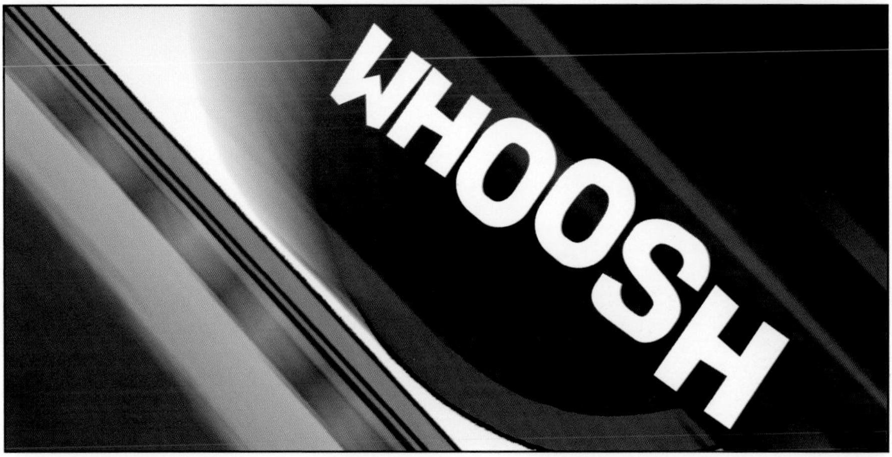
WHOOSH

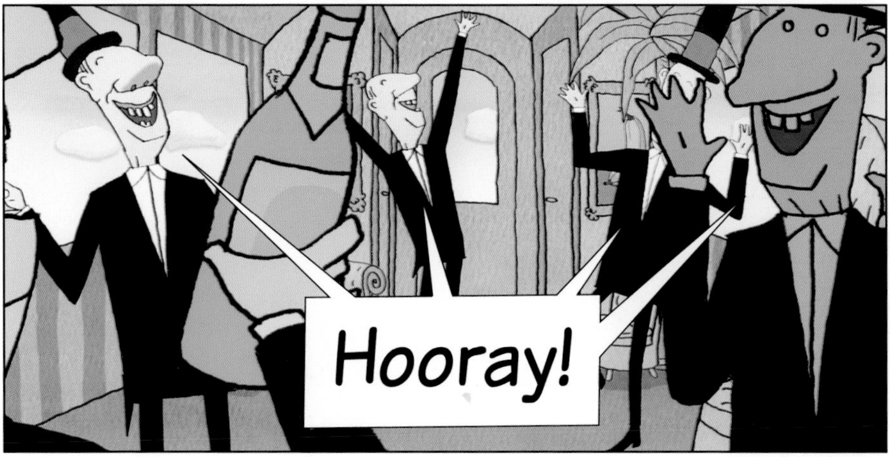
Hooray!

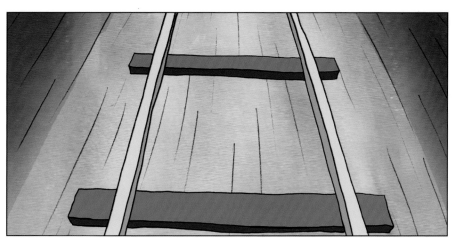

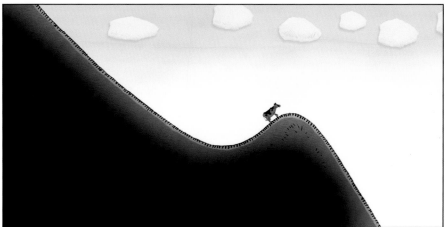

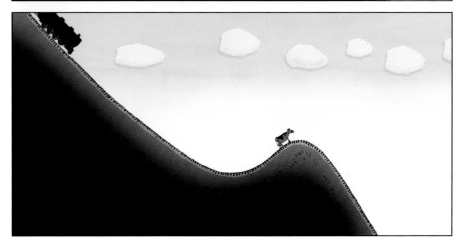

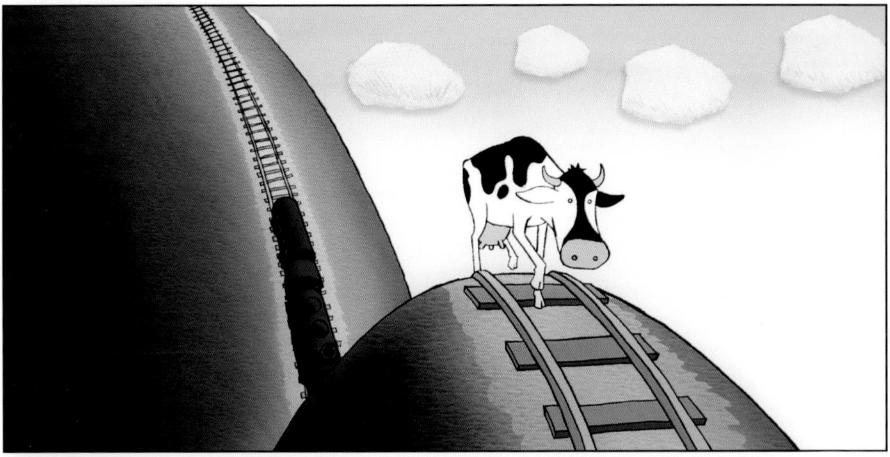

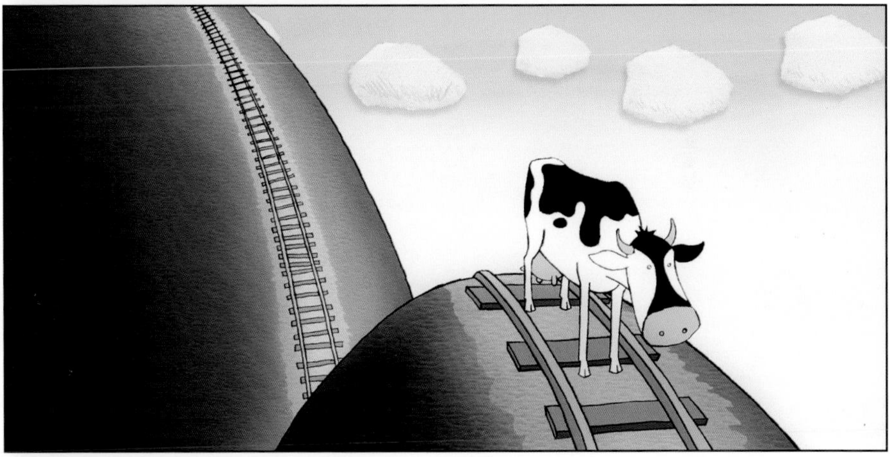

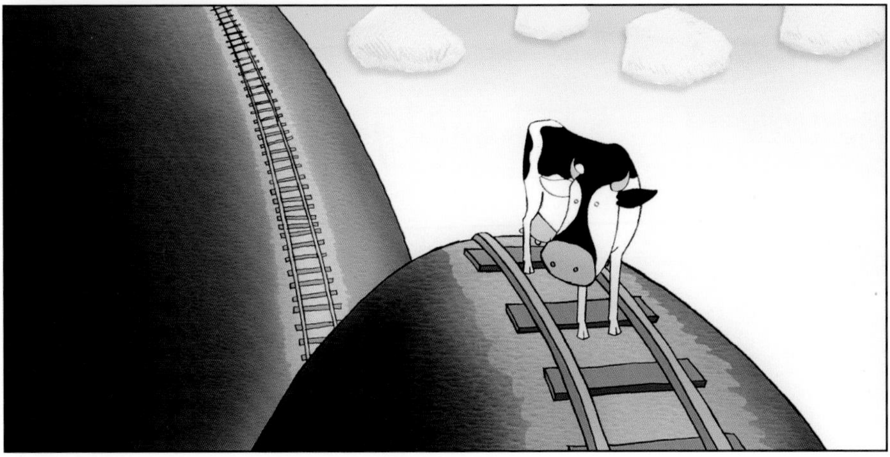

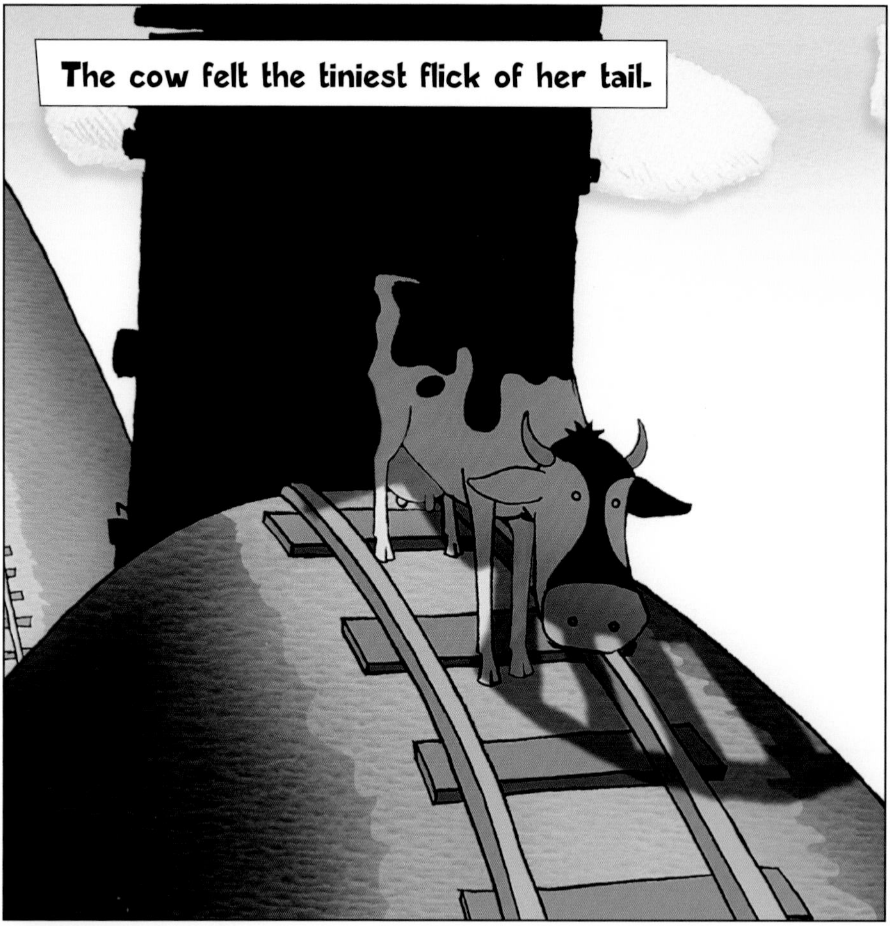
The cow felt the tiniest flick of her tail.

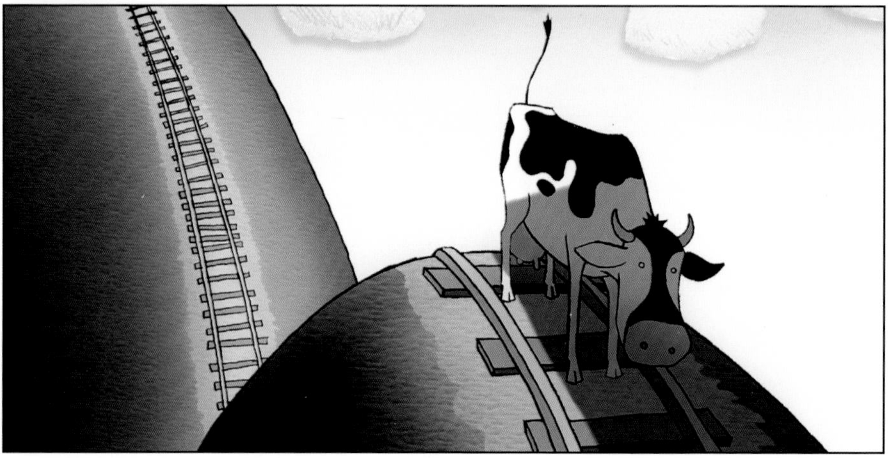

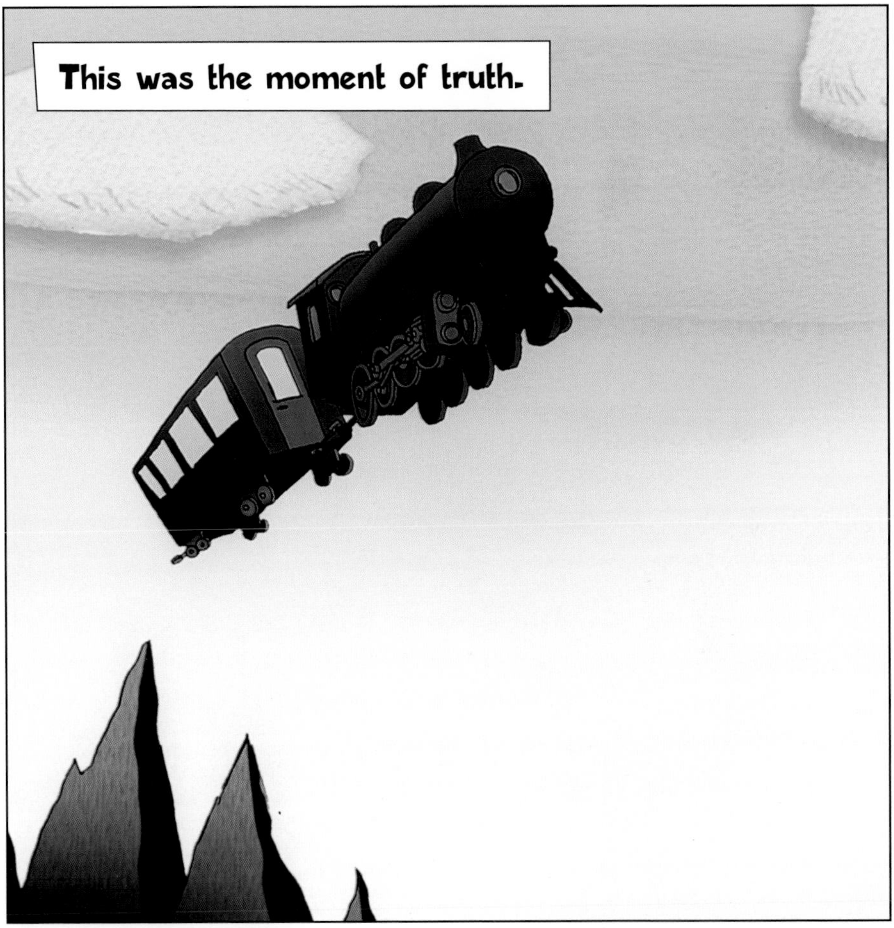
This was the moment of truth.
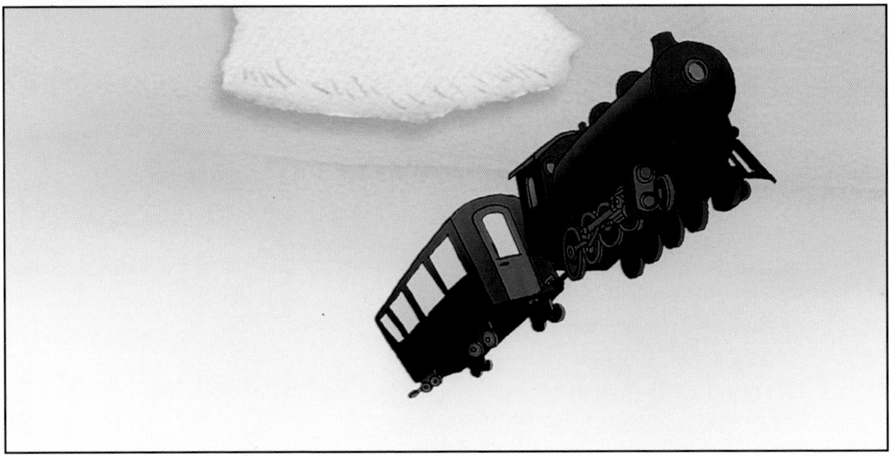

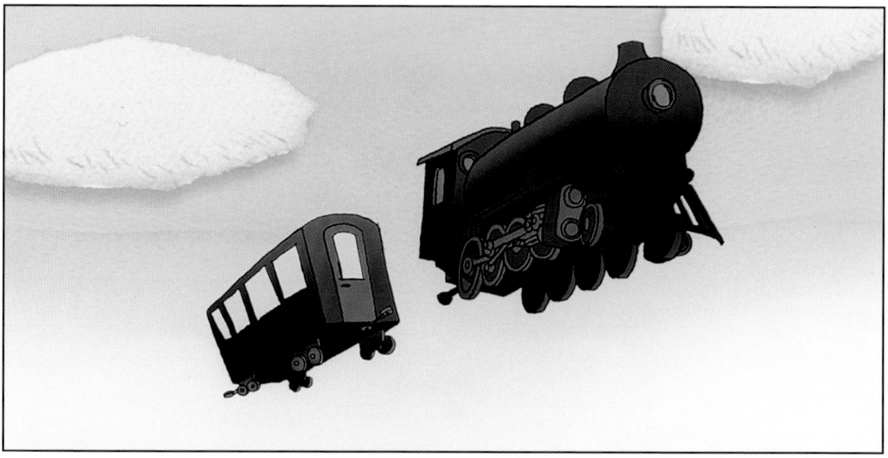

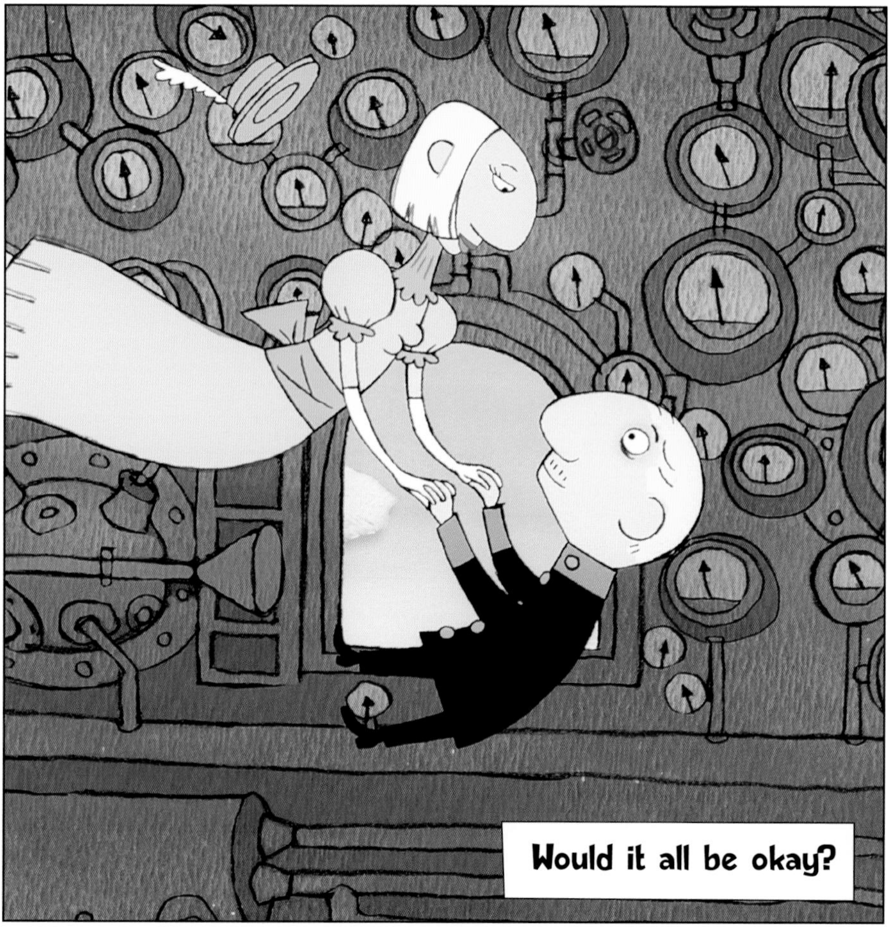
Would it all be okay?

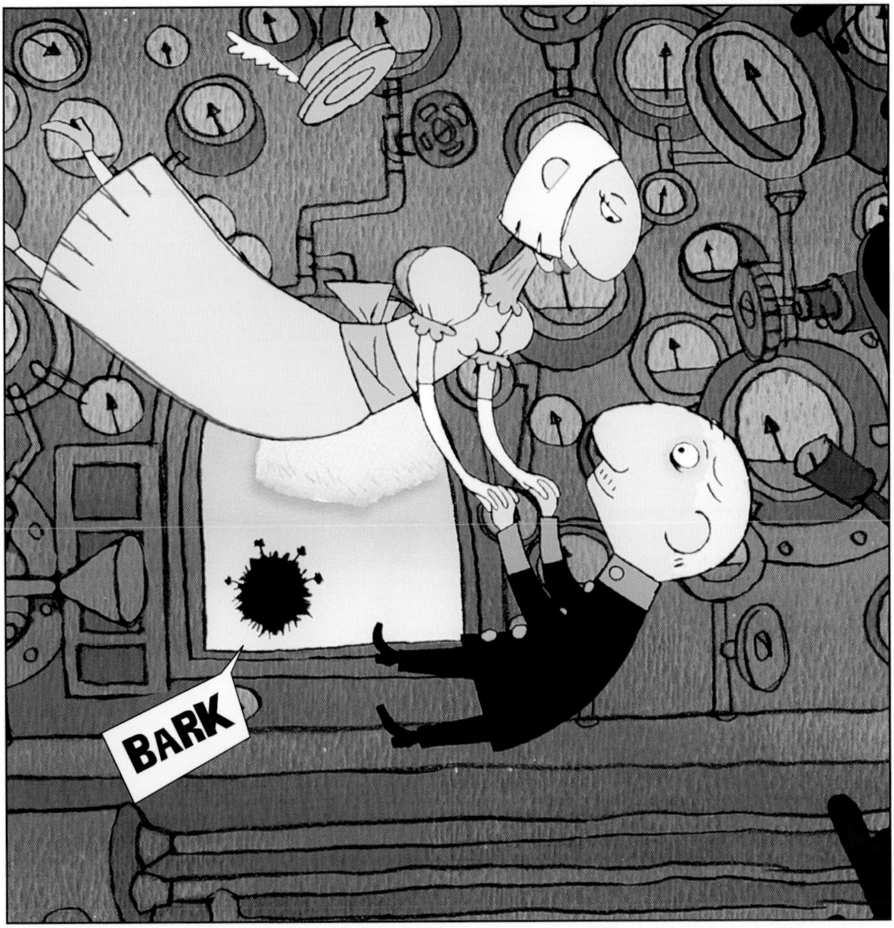
BARK

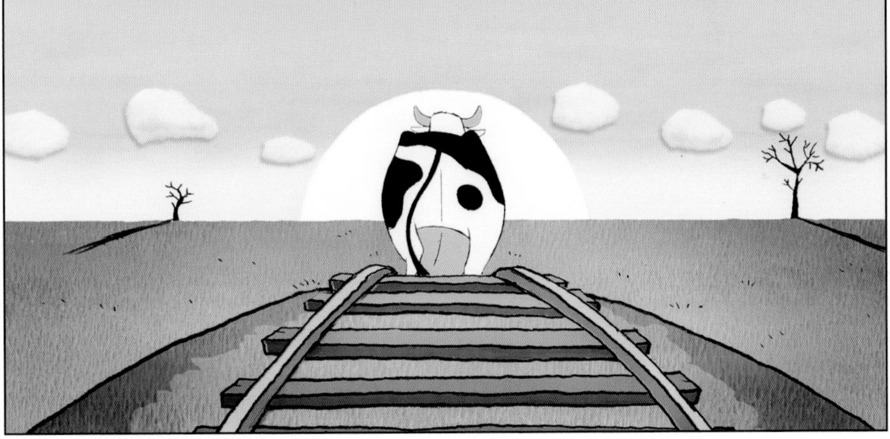

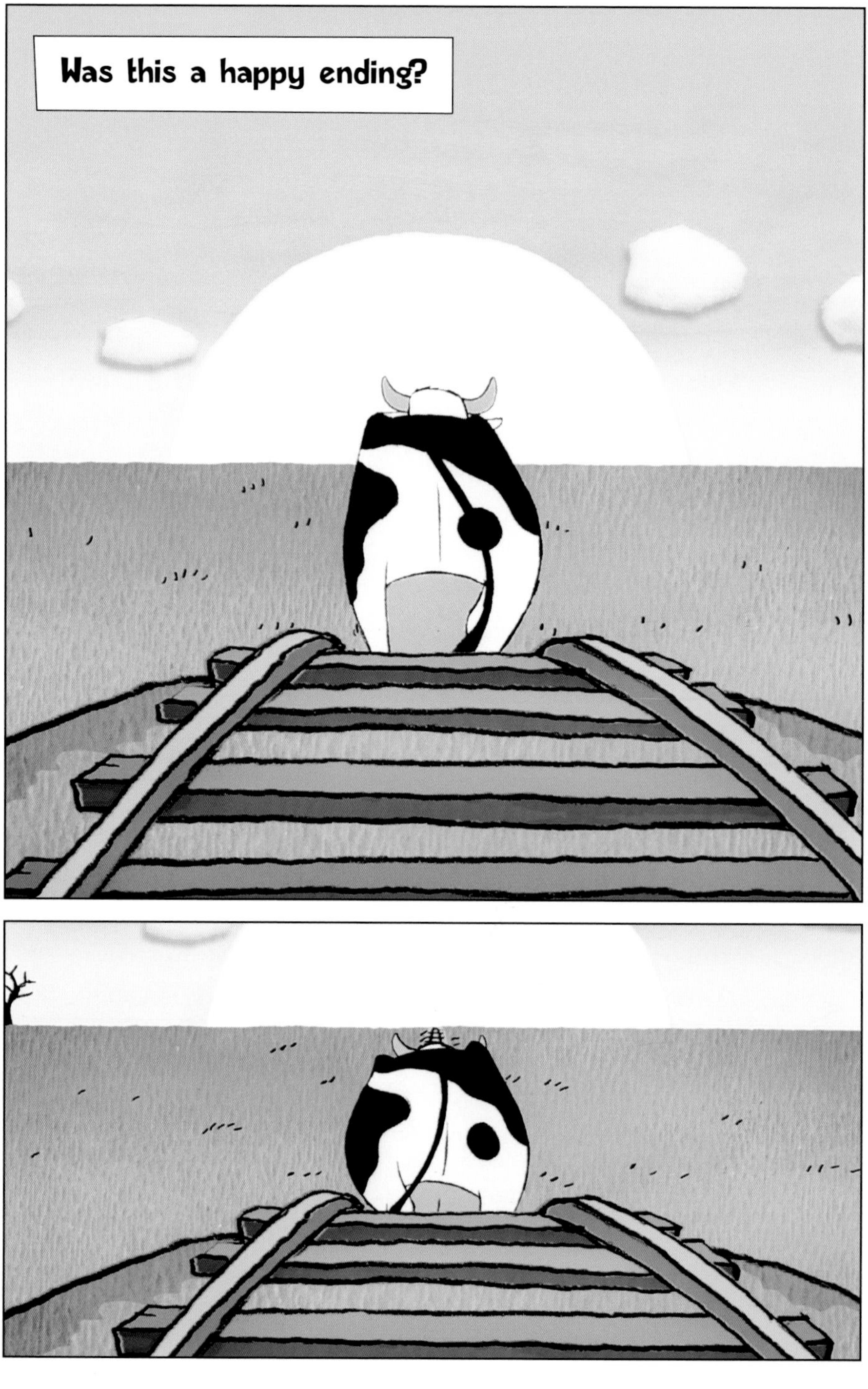
Was this a happy ending?

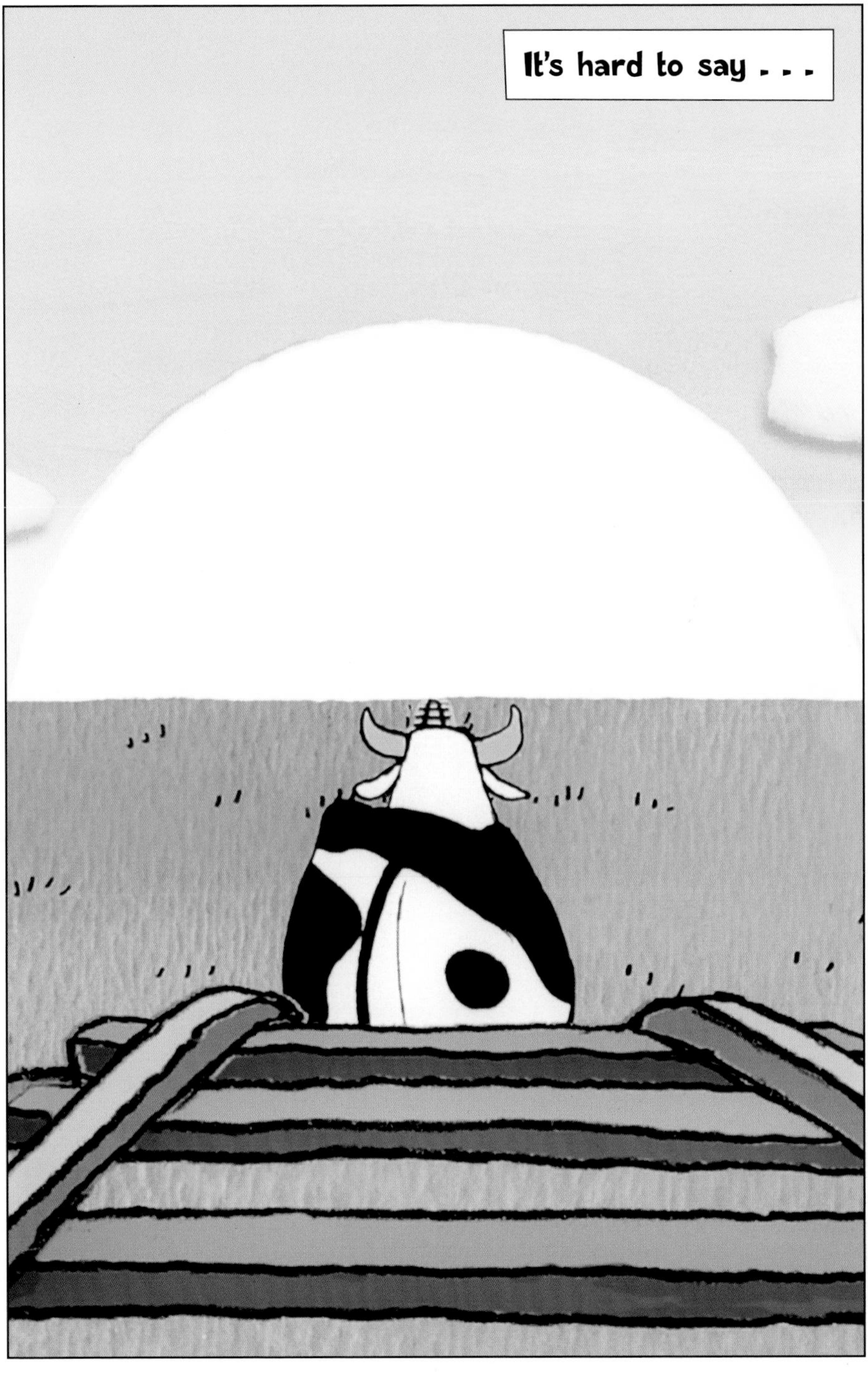
It's hard to say . . .

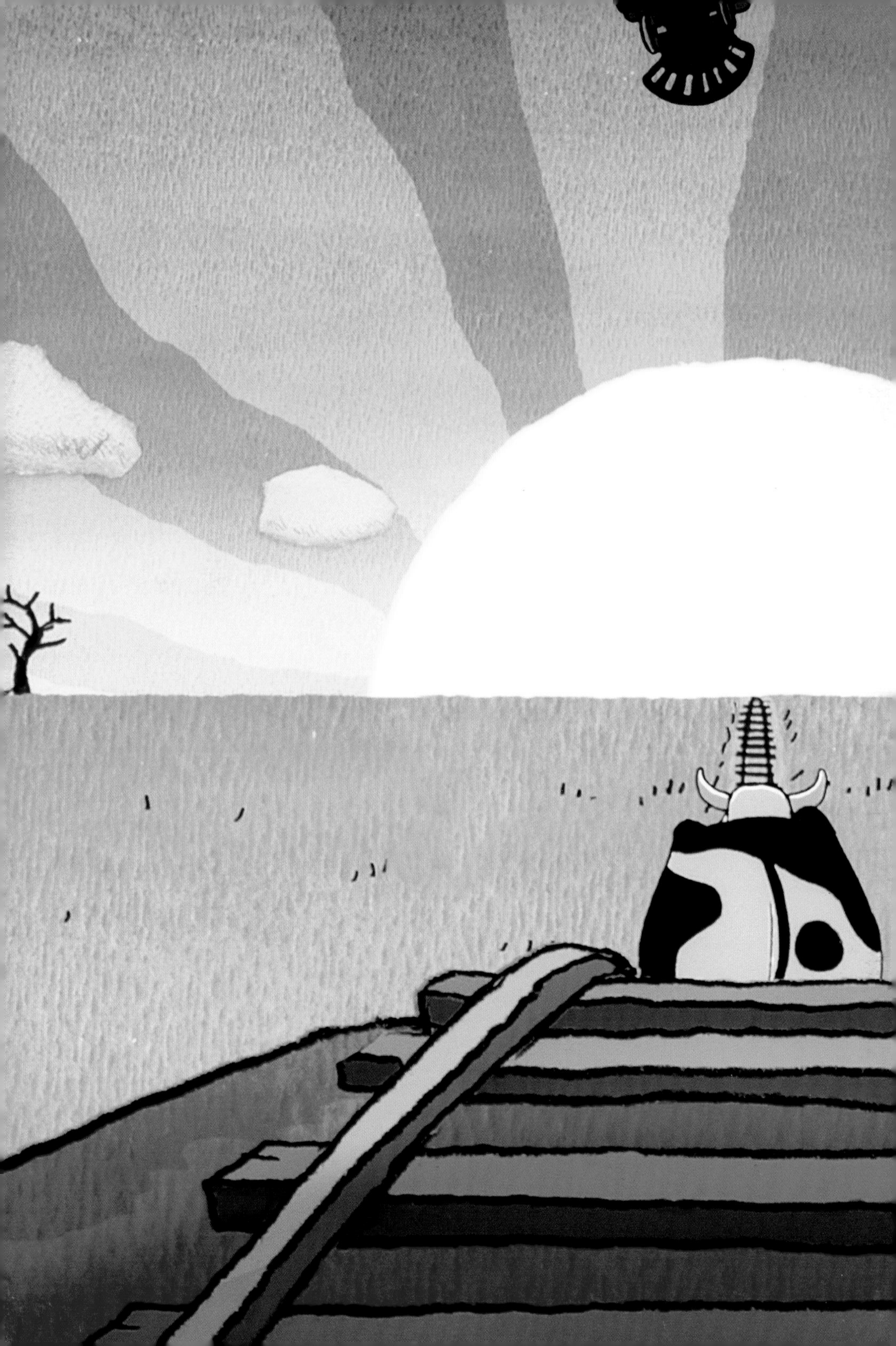

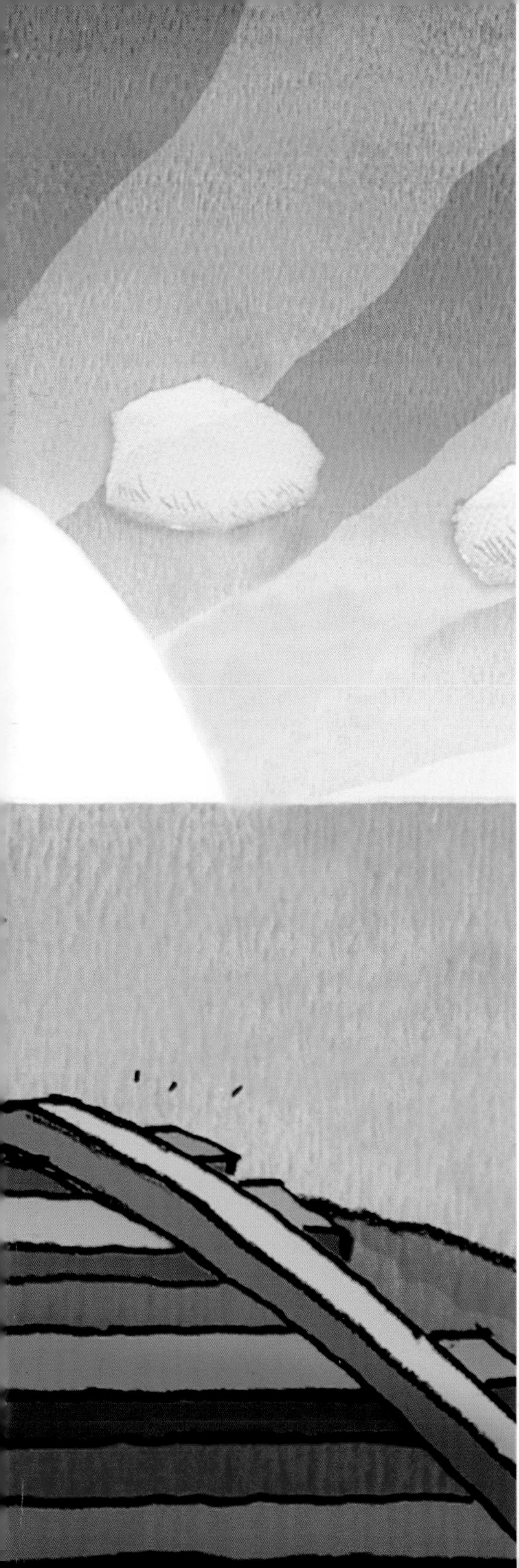

But for the cow,
it was a glorious
sunset.

A FIREFLY BOOK

Published under license from the National Film Board of Canada by Firefly Books Ltd. 2019
Story and characters © 2009 Cordell Barker
Book design and adaptation © 2019 Firefly Books Ltd.

Adapted from the animated short film *Runaway* © 2009 National Film Board of Canada

First printing

Library of Congress Control Number: 2019937753

Library and Archives Canada Cataloguing in Publication
Title: Runaway / Cordell Barker ; adapted by Sarah Howden.
Names: Howden, Sarah, author. | Barker, Cordell.
Series: National Film Board of Canada collection.
Description: Series statement: National Film Board of Canada collection
Identifiers: Canadiana 20190095148 | ISBN 9780228100799 (hardcover)
Classification: LCC PS8615.O93 R86 2019 | DDC jC813/.6—dc23

Published in the United States by
Firefly Books (U.S.) Inc.
P.O. Box 1338, Ellicott Station
Buffalo, New York 14205

Published in Canada by
Firefly Books Ltd.
50 Staples Avenue, Unit 1
Richmond Hill, Ontario L4B 0A7

Interior Design: Sam Tse

Printed in China

 We acknowledge the financial support of the Government of Canada.

The NFB is Canada's public producer of award-winning creative documentaries, auteur animation, interactive stories and participatory experiences. NFB producers are embedded in communities across the country, from St. John's to Vancouver, working with talented creators on innovative and socially relevant projects. The NFB is a leader in gender equity in film and digital media production, and is working to strengthen Indigenous-led production, guided by the recommendations of Canada's Truth and Reconciliation Commission. NFB productions have won over 7,000 awards, including 24 Canadian Screen Awards, 18 Webbys, 12 Oscars and more than 100 Genies. To access NFB works, visit NFB.ca or download its apps for mobile devices.